W. H. Davenport (William Henry Davenport Adams

In the Far East

W. H. Davenport (William Henry Davenport Adams

In the Far East

ISBN/EAN: 9783742897077

Manufactured in Europe, USA, Canada, Australia, Japa

Cover: Foto ©Andreas Hilbeck / pixelio.de

Manufactured and distributed by brebook publishing software
(www.brebook.com)

W. H. Davenport (William Henry Davenport Adams

In the Far East

IN THE FAR EAST.

IN THE FAR EAS

A Narrative of Exploration and Adventure

IN COCHIN-CHINA, CAMBODIA, LAOS, AND SIAM.

.

BY THE AUTHOR OF

"*The Arctic World,*" "*The Mediterranean Illustrated,*"
&c. &c.

WITH TWENTY-EIGHT FULL-PAGE ILLUSTRATIONS.

LONDON: THOMAS NELSON AND SONS.
EDINBURGH AND NEW YORK.

1879.

Contents.

IN THE FAR EAST.

CHAPTER I.

THROUGH LAOS TO CHINA.

CONSIDERABLE portion of the Indo-Chinese peninsula is occupied by the extensive country of Cambodia, or Camboja, known to the natives as *Kan-pou-chi.* It extends from lat. 8° 47′ to 15° N., along the basin of the Mekong, Makiang, or Cambodia river; and is bounded on the north by Laos; on the south, by the Gulf of Siam and the China Sea; on the east, by Cochin-China; and on the west, by Siam. Formerly it was independent; but since 1809 it has been included within the empire of Annam, except the province of Battabang, which belongs to the kingdom of Siam. But since the French established themselves at Saigon in 1858, and have gradually

obtained a controlling power in Annam (or Cochin-China), their influence has also extended to Cambodia.

The largest river of Cambodia, and of the whole Indo-Chinese peninsula, is the Mekong, Makiang, or Cambodia, which, rising in the mountains of China, under the name of the Lan-tsan-kiang, flows in a south-easterly direction across the province of Yunnan; thence, under the name of the Kiou-long, traverses the territory of Laos; and afterwards, as the Mekong, intersects Cambodia, dividing the Annam portion from that which belongs to Siam; separates into several branches, and finally falls into the China Sea, after a fertilizing course of about fifteen hundred miles. Its two principal mouths are those of the Japanese and Oubequum channels. There are several smaller mouths, however, the southernmost of which is situated in lat. 9° 30′ N., and long. 106° 20′ E.

Very little was known of this great river until the French had made themselves masters of Saigon. It has since been explored in parts of its course by M. Mouhot, Lieutenant Garnier, and others. The country which it waters possesses many features of interest; and the scenery through which it flows is often of a romantic and beautiful character. The manners and customs of the people dwelling on its banks are not unworthy of consideration ; and we propose, therefore, to carry the reader with us on a voyage up this magnificent stream,—penetrating, under the guidance of Lieutenant Garnier, into hitherto unexplored parts of Cambodia, and even into China itself.

In 1866 the French Government determined on despatching an expedition to explore the upper valley of the great Cambodian river, and placed it in charge of M. de Lagrée, a captain in the French navy. M. Thorel, a surgeon, was attached to it as botanist ; M. Delaporte, as artist ; Dr. Joubert, as physician and geologist ; and among the other members were Lieutenant Garnier, to whose record of the expedition we are about to be indebted, and M. de Carné. After a visit to Ongcor, the capital of the ancient kingdom of the Khmers, with those vast memorials of antiquity described so graphically by M. Mouhot, the expedition proceeded to ascend the great river, passing the busy villages of Compong Luong and Pnom Penh—the latter the residence of the king of Cambodia. Here they aban-

doned the gun-brigs which had brought them from
Saigon, and embarked themselves and their stores
on board boats better fitted for river navigation.

These boats or canoes are manned, according to
their size, by a crew of six to ten men. Each is
armed with a long bamboo, one end of which terminates with an iron hook, the other with a small
fork. The men take up their station on a small
platform in the fore part of the boat, plant their
bamboos against some projection on the river-bank,
tree or stone, and then march towards the stern;
returning afterwards on the opposite side to repeat
the process. This strange kind of circular motion
suffices to impel the boat at the rate of a man
walking at full speed, when the boatmen are skil-
ful at their work, and the river-bank is straight
and well defined. The master's attention is wholly
occupied, meanwhile, in keeping the bow of the
canoe in the direction of the current, or rather
slightly headed towards the shore. It is obvious
that such a mode of navigation is liable to many
interruptions, and cannot be commended on the
score of swiftness or convenience.

On the 13th of July the canoes took their
departure from Cratich, and soon afterwards arrived

at Sombor. They then effected the passage of the
rapids of Sombor-Sombor—no great difficulty being
experienced, owing to the rise of the waters. Beyond
this point the broad bed of the great river was
encumbered with a multitude of islands, low and
green, while the banks were covered with magnificent forests. The voyagers noticed here some trees
of great value—the yao; the ban-courg, the wood
of which makes capital oars; and the lam-xe, which
should be highly prized by the European cabinet-
makers.

On the 16th of July the voyagers again fell in
with a series of formidable rapids. The sharp and
clearly-defined shores of the islands which had
hitherto enclosed the arm of the river they were
navigating were suddenly effaced. The Cambodia
was covered with innumerable clumps of trees, half
under water; its muddy torrent rolled impetuously
through a thousand canals, forming an inextricable
labyrinth. Huge blocks of sandstone rose at intervals along the left bank, and indicated that strata
of the same rock extended across the river-bed. At
a considerable distance from the shore the poles of
the boatmen found a depth of fully ten feet; and
it was with extreme difficulty the canoes made way

against the strong, fierce current, which in some confined channels attained a velocity of five miles an hour.

Storms of wind and rain contributed to render the voyage more wearisome and the progress slower. It was no easy task at night to find a secure haven for the boats; and the sudden floods of the little streams at the mouth of which the voyagers sought shelter, several times subjected them to the risk of being carried away during their sleep, and cast all unexpectedly into the mid-current of the great river. They slept on board their boats, because the roof was some protection from the furious rains; but these soon soaked through the mats and leaves of which it was composed. The weather was warm, and thus these douche-baths were not wholly insupportable; and when the voyagers could not sleep, they found some consolation in admiring the fantastic illumination which the incessant lightnings kindled in the gloomy arcades of the forest, and in listening to the peals of thunder, repeated by a thousand echoes, and mingling with the hoarse continuous growl of the angry waters.

Such are some of the features of the navigation of the lower part of the Cambodia. But our limits

compel us to pass over several chapters of Lieutenant
Garnier's narrative, and to take it up after the
voyagers had crossed the boundaries of Siam and
Cambodia and entered Laos.

Lieutenant Garnier describes the Laotians as generally well made and robust. Their physiognomy,
he says, is characterized by a singular combination
of cunning and apathy, benevolence and timorous-
ness. Their eyes are less regular, their cheeks less
prominent, the nose straighter, than is the case
with other peoples of Mongolian origin ; and but for
their much paler complexion, which closely approaches that of the Chinese, we should be tempted
to credit them with a considerable admixture of
Hindu blood. The male Laotian shaves his head,
and, like the Siamese, preserves only a small tuft
of very short hair on the summit. He dresses himself tastefully, and can wear the finest stuffs with
ease and dignity. He chooses always the liveliest
colours ; and the effect of a group of Laotians, with
the brilliant hues of their costume set off by their
copper-tinted skin, is very striking. The common
people wear an exceedingly simple garb—the langouti, a piece of cotton stuff passed between the
legs and around the waist. For those of higher

rank the langouti is of silk; and is frequently accompanied by a small vest buttoned over the chest, with very narrow sleeves, and another piece of silk folded round the waist as a girdle, or round the neck as a scarf. Head-gear and foot-gear are things little used in Laos; but the labourers and boatmen, when working or rowing under a burning sun, protect the head with an immense straw hat, almost flat, much like a parasol. Personages of high rank, when they are in "full dress," wear a kind of slipper, which appears to inconvenience them greatly, and is thrown off at the earliest opportunity.

Most of the Laotians tattoo themselves on the stomach or legs, though the practice is much more prevalent in the north than in the south. The Laotian women do not wear much more clothing than their husbands. The langouti, instead of being brought up between the legs, is fastened round the waist, and allowed to hang down like a short tight petticoat below the knees. Generally, a second piece of stuff is worn over the bosom, and thrown back across either the right or left shoulder. The hair, always of a splendid jetty blackness, is twisted up in a chignon on the top of the head, and kept in its place by a small strip of cotton or plaited straw, frequently embellished with a few flowers. Every woman ornaments her neck, arms, and legs with rings of gold, silver, or copper, sometimes heaped one upon another in considerable quantity. The very poor are content with belts of cotton or silk; to which, in the case of children, are suspended little amulets given by the priests as talismans against witchcraft or remedies against disease.

Strictly speaking, polygamy does not exist in Laos. Only the well-to-do indulge in the embarrassing luxury of more wives than one; and even with these a favoured individual is recognized as the lawful spouse.

Unhappily, slavery prevails, as it does in Siam and Cambodia. A debtor may be enslaved, by judicial confiscation; but the "peculiar institution" is chiefly recruited from the wild tribes in the eastern provinces. The slaves are employed in tilling the fields, and in domestic labours; they are treated with great kindness. They often live so intimately and so familiarly with their masters, that, but for their long hair and characteristic physiognomy, it would be difficult to distinguish them in the midst of a Laotian "interior."

The Laotians are a slothful people, and, when not rich enough to own slaves, leave the best part of the day's work to be done by the women, who not only perform the household labour, but pound the rice, till the fields, paddle the canoes. Hunting and fishing are almost the only occupations reserved for the stronger sex.

We have not space to describe all the engines employed for catching fish, which, next to rice, is the principal food of all the riverine populations of the Mekong valley, and is furnished by the great river in almost inexhaustible quantities. The most common are large tubes of bamboo and ratan, having one or more funnel-shaped necks, the edges of which prevent the fish from escaping after they have once entered. These apparatus are firmly attached, with their openings towards the current, to a tree on the river-bank, or, by means of some heavy stones, are completely submerged. Every second or third day their owner visits them, and empties them of their finny victims. The Laotians also make use of an ingenious system of floats, which support a row of hooks, and realize the European "fishing by line," without the help of the fisherman. There are various other methods adopted, such as the net and the harpoon; and in the employment of all these the Laotians display considerable activity and address.

Let us now accompany our French voyagers in their further ascent of the river. As we have already hinted, its navigation is not without its inconveniences, and even its dangers. One evening, for example, they dropped anchor at the mouth of a small stream which, in foam and spray, came tumbling down from the mountains of Cambodia. After supper they lay down to rest on the mats which covered the deck of their vessels. Black was the sky, hot and oppressive the air; all around were visible the portents of a coming storm. The distant roar of the hurricane failed, however, to disturb the sleepers, who were spent and overcome with the fatigues of the day. But at last they were wakened effectually by a "thunder-plump." which quickly flooded their canoes, and drove them upon deck.

In the midst of the elemental disorder, they became aware of a hoarse growling sound; the waters were violently agitated, and a great crest of foam rapidly advanced towards their feeble barks.

In a few moments it was upon them. It swept clean over the voyagers and their canoes, and those of the latter which had been carelessly moored were borne down the rushing tide. At first an indescribable disorder prevailed; cries of distress rose in every direction; the canoes dashed violently against one another, or came into collision with uprooted trunks floating on the surface of the storm-tossed waters. Fortunately, the danger was quickly over; and as every boat had contrived to grapple some branch or rock, the voyagers discovered at daybreak that, whatever injuries these had sustained, no lives had been lost. The furious gale they had heard in the distance had raised the waters some twelve feet during the night; but the inundation subsided as rapidly as it had risen.

Under the shade of wide-branching trees, and closely hugging the shore, the expedition continued its voyage. The neighbouring forests were remarkable for their luxuriant vegetation; troops of apes and squirrels of various species gambolled among the mighty trees, among which rose conspicuous the superb yao, the king of these forests, the trunk of which shoots up, free from knot or bough, to a height of eighty or one hundred feet; and out of which the Laotians hollow their piraguas. In the morning a wild beast now and then came down to the river to drink; and night was rendered hideous by the cries and trumpetings of deer, and tigers, and elephants.

At length the voyagers came within hearing of the tremendous roar of the Khon cataract. Their boatmen, brisker than on ordinary occasions, hauled or propelled their vessels through a very labyrinth of rocks, submerged trees, and prostrate trunks still clinging to earth by their many roots. They knew that their hard labour was nearly at an end, and that at Khon the expedition would dismiss them, as fresh boats would be required above the cataract. As for their homeward voyage, what was it? To ascend the river had been the work of a week; the swift current would bear them back in less than a day.

The cataract of Khon is really a series of magnificent falls, of which one of the grandest is caused by the confluence of the Papheng. There, in the midst of rocks and grassy islets, an enormous sheet of water leaps headlong from a height of seventy feet, to fall back in floods of foam, again to descend

from crag to crag, and finally glide away beneath
the dense vegetation of the forest. As the river at
this point is about one thousand yards in width, the
effect is singularly striking. But still more impos-
ing is the Salaphe fall, which extends over a breadth
of a mile and a half, at the very foot of the mountains. In order to examine it at leisure, Lieutenant
Garnier engaged a Laotian to conduct him to an
island lying just above it. Before starting, the
guide made certain preparations, of which Garnier
could not understand the necessity, in spite of the
Laotian's efforts to explain them. Rolling up about
his waist the light langouti, he plastered his feet
and legs with a composition of lime and areca juice.
This precaution proved to be far from useless; for,
on landing on the island, they found the soil covered
with thousands of leeches, some no larger than
needles, but others two inches and a half to three
inches in length. On the approach of the strangers,
they reared themselves erect upon each dead leaf
and blade of grass; they leaped, so to speak, upon
them from every side. The thick coating which
the Laotian guide had so prudently assumed preserved him from their bites; but Garnier, in a few
moments, was victimized by dozens of these blood-

suckers, which crawled up his legs and bled him in spite of all his efforts. He found it impossible to get rid of his determined antagonists; for one leech which he tore off, two fresh assailants seized upon him. Glad was he when he caught sight of a tall tree. He made towards it, scaled its trunk, and, when out of reach of his foes, set to work to deliver himself from the creatures which were feasting at his expense. Throwing off his clothes, he removed the leeches one by one, though it was not without difficulty that he loosened their hold. Even his waistband had not arrested their march, for he found that one audacious persecutor had actually reached his chest.

He felt more than repaid, however, for all his sufferings, when he arrived within sight of the cataract. With a breadth of two thousand yards, a prodigious mass of water came down in blinding foam, roaring like a furious sea when it breaks against an iron-bound coast. At another point, the flood was divided into eight or ten different cascades by as many projecting crags, richly clothed in leafage and vegetation. Beyond, nothing could be seen but one immense rapid,—a roaring, tumultuous deluge! The sandstone blocks and boulders which

encumbered the river-bed were completely hidden
by the whirl and eddy of the waves; and their
position could be detected only by the foam on the
surface, or the vapour floating wreath-like in the
air. Further still, a few black points, a few ridges
of rock, and a chain of small islets, stretched across
to the opposite bank, which it was impossible to
approach, and where, apparently, the cataract seemed
to attain its greatest fury.   Such was the great fall
of Salaphe,—a scene of sublime grandeur, convey-
ing the idea of everlasting strength and power.

While preparing to continue their ascent of the
river, Lieutenant Garnier and his companions
visited Bassac, one of the most important towns in
Laos.   It is situated in the heart of the richest
tropical scenery; and the members of the expedition
found it impossible to ramble in any direction without coming upon some fresh and beautiful landscape, or some object of the highest interest.   The
mountains which surround Bassac are clothed to
their very summits with vegetation; and down the
shadowy glens which furrow their rugged sides
sparkle bright, pure streams on their way to the
all-absorbing Mekong.   The people of Bassac are

a mild and peaceable race, and they received the
strangers with cordial hospitality. The time was
spent most agreeably in paying and receiving visits;
in excursions among the beautiful scenery of the
neighbourhood, the choicest "bits" of which they
transferred to their sketch-books; in studying the
manners and customs of the inhabitants; and in
essaying their skill as marksmen against the wild
denizens of the forest.

The larger game are generally caught by the
hunters of Bassac in nets or snares. The chase on
a grand scale is almost unknown. In the forests,
however, the hunters sometimes call in the elephant
to their assistance; they are thus able to get close
to the wished-for prey, as the latter do not take
alarm at the approach of an animal so well known.
Lieutenant Garnier tells us that he enjoyed his
sport in a modest fashion. Sometimes he spent
whole days in traversing the dried-up swamps, in the
shade of dense masses of trees bound together inex-
tricably by every kind of liana and parasite. To
such places resort numerous companies of peacocks
and wild fowl during the hot season; but their
pursuit is always difficult, and frequently dangerous.
Indeed, the Laotians cherish a belief that the tiger

and the peacock are always found in the same
localities.

One evening, seated at the foot of a tamarisk-tree,
the fruit of which a troop of squirrels was busily
crunching among the branches overhead, Garnier and
his comrade, Dr. Thorel, took counsel together; with
the conclusion that, on the day following, they
would undertake a mountain excursion, and boldly
attempt to scale one of the most elevated peaks.
Accordingly, at dawn they started, attended by their
usual escort—a native, christened Luiz.

With swift feet they crossed the rice-plantations
and marshes that separated them from the foot of
the mountains; and by a narrow winding track
reached the bed of a dried-up torrent, where they
halted for a brief rest. Thence, plunging into the
forest, they slowly climbed the precipitous heights,
occasionally confronted by a rugged steep, or an
immense mass of rock that seemed likely to baffle
all their aspirations, but was eventually conquered
by combined skill and resolution. The forest soon
changed its character; the rarefaction of the air forced
itself upon their notice; the daring adventurers rose
above the clouds and vapours of the plain. On

PEACOCK HUNTING.

arriving at a narrow ledge of table-land they halted
for breakfast. The first requisite was fresh water;
rare enough at that season of the year, and at such
a height! Close beside them, however, was the
channel of a spent burn; and a careful search
among the rocks revealed to them a pool, sheltered
from wind and sun, brimming with crystal water,
—and tenanted, moreover, by some mountain-eels,
small but delicious. The pool being very shallow,
a supply of the eels was soon obtained.

It did not take long to kindle a fire. The eels
were dexterously grilled; and a savoury and sub-
stantial repast concluded with a dessert of wild
bananas. Refreshed and invigorated, the mountain-
climbers resumed their enterprise; and along a
narrow crest, so narrow that two persons could not
walk abreast, made their way through a labyrinth
of vegetation. With watchful eye, and hand on
trigger, they advanced. Suddenly a strayed peacock flew in front of them; but as their position
was unfavourable for taking aim, they allowed it to
pass by. They reached at last a kind of natural
staircase, the ascent of which was rendered incon-
venient by the showers of pebbles, loosened by their
feet, which rolled to right and left over the preci-

pice. All at once further progress apparently was
rendered impossible by a mass of withered brushwood; which, on examination, proved to be the den,
happily deserted, of a wild boar.

Beyond this point the crest or ridge grew sharper
and sharper; the shattered and accumulated rocks
were held together only by the lianas which close-
clasped them; and the adventurers were forced to
crawl on their hands and knees, holding on by
plant or crag. At length the brave effort was
crowned with success. They gained the mountain-
top, and enjoyed a panorama of wonderful beauty,
in which peaks and forests blended their various
hues, and wide green plains expanded in the golden
sunshine, and the pagodas of Bassac rose like island-
pinnacles out of a sea of verdure. The glorious
picture, in all its variety of form and glow of
colouring, was one on which the eye of man had
never before rested; it was a picture of abounding
fertility as well as of beauty and grandeur, and
suggested the idea of almost inexhaustible resources,
which in some future time may be developed by
the enterprise and civilization of the West.

In the course of their descent the explorers
gained a broken ridge of rock, overshadowed by the

MOUNTAIN-PEAK NEAR BASSAO.

branches of a stately tree, the roots of which clung round the weather-worn stones, and seemed to hold them together. At their approach, a swarm—we might almost say a cloud—of green pigeons whirled and fluttered out of the depths of the green foliage; returning to their resting-places after a few aerial evolutions. The ground beneath was strewn with small fruit, to which the pigeons are extremely partial; and showers continually fell about the explorers' heads, loosened by the movement of the restless birds. With a little patience, they brought down half a dozen of the feathered spoilers; and then, through the forest shadows and down the mountain-declivities, they pursued their homeward march.

The following evening, Garnier and Dr. Thorel were invited to join a young Laotian in his walk. The latter led them across a pleasant breadth of garden-ground to an open space, strewn here and there with ashes and the refuse of wood-fires. Behind a clump of tall bamboos, some fifty spectators, seated in an oval ring, surrounded a couple of wrestlers, and displayed a lively interest in the various phases of their strife. At a few paces distant, three men were engaged in rekindling a fire

. which had died out for lack of fuel. Some bonzes, or priests, clothed in full long robes of yellow stuff, were viewing the spectacle from afar, or wending their way towards the neighbouring pagoda. Two or three women crouched on the ground, amidst baskets of fruit and large earthen vessels full of rice-wine, intended as refreshment for the spectators or the heated athletes.

Among the bystanders was conspicuous a Laotian, attired in a langouti, and silken vest of dazzling colours, and sheltered by a parasol held over his head by a boy standing in the rear, who warmly encouraged one of the combatants, while a portion of the assembly evidently backed his antagonist. The struggle was protracted. Betting took place vigorously, and considerable sums were wagered on both sides. The white men seated themselves apart, in order to study in all its details a scene so full of animation. It was impossible not to admire the suppleness of the two athletes,—robust young men, trained to the combat from their very infancy; impossible not to take an interest in the skill and agility with which they eluded or endeavoured to surprise one another. Sometimes they paused, face to face, and regarded each other

FUNERAL CEREMONY OF THE LAOTIANS.

with fixed gaze, slightly curving their loins or shoulders ; a moment, and they leaped from end to end of the arena, assuming theatrical attitudes—and, when occasion offered, dealing a vigorous blow of the fist which reddened the sun-bronzed skin.

Their Laotian friend informed our travellers that they were witnessing nothing less than a funeral ceremony! In Laos, cremation is the universal custom ; and the mortuary rites of a Laotian of rank generally terminate with a gladiatorial combat, at the conclusion and on the very site of the process of cremation.

The national rule is, that the corpse of a Laotian mandarin shall be preserved for several days in its shroud within the proper mortuary-hut. Friends and kinsmen assemble therein, and console themselves as best they may with abundant eating and drinking; a custom which prevails elsewhere than in Laos! It does not appear that the Laotians regard death with any particular apprehension. Their special anxiety is to prevent the evil spirits from obtaining possession of the souls of the dead, and playing them malignant tricks. During the day these spirits will not attempt anything ; but at night they gain courage, and to shelter the deceased from their manœuvres seems to be no easy task. However, by means of numerous prayers, and more particularly by keeping up a tremendous clamour, it is generally possible, the Laotians believe, to avert their disastrous influence.

For this purpose all the bonzes of the neighbourhood are summoned; and taking up positions around the bier, they chant aloud their invocations. By day, and especially by night, the family assist them in keeping watch. The women decorate the coffin with floral offerings, as well as with ornaments of wax intended to facilitate combustion. The men, armed with gongs, tomtoms, and any other instrument they can seize upon, accompany, as noisily as possible, the chants of the bonzes. "Harmony" is not the object aimed at; but to secure the maximum of noise.

When the day appointed for the final ceremony arrives, the uproar is redoubled at early morn, as a signal to the friends and relatives of the departed, who make their appearance in full costume.

A procession is then arranged for the purpose of carrying the corpse to the place of burning. The bonzes lead the way, the seniors coming last. Then follows the coffin, supported on the shoulders of a

dozen young men, and surmounted by a kind of
bamboo canopy, embellished with flowers and foliage, and destined, like the coffin, to be consumed on
the funeral pyre. The men march next, with the
wealthiest and most influential of the kinsmen of
the deceased at their head. The rear is brought up
by the women and children, carrying long bamboos
ornamented with banderoles of various colours, which
are planted in the ground during the process of
cremation.

The pile is reared at one extremity of the burial-
ground, where bamboo poles and the trunks of aged
palms have been linked together with long lianas to
form a kind of aerial barrier against the invasion of
the evil spirits. It is composed of pieces of wood
of equal length, carefully arranged in intercrossed
layers, and it rises to the height of a man's shoulders,
so that the bearers, passing half to one side and half
to the other, can deposit the coffin without effort.
The men gather round in a circle; the women stand
a little in the rear. The bonzes recite their prayers,
and receive once more the offerings which the relatives of the deceased never fail to bring for them
and their pagoda; after which the chief priest
mounts the pile, and standing erect, with hands

extended over the coffin, pronounces with a loud voice a concluding prayer.

As soon as he has descended, the attendants set fire to the resinous materials placed under the pile. A dazzling jet of flame shoots aloft, and soon envelopes the coffin. The ornaments are consumed in quick succession; the pile breaks down in a mass of flame and smoke; and into the midst falls the corpse, released from the charred and burning coffin. Yet, painful as this spectacle seems, no native exhibits the slightest emotion. The work of combustion is allowed to complete itself, and no one touches the ashes of humanity throughout the day. The women depart, while the men follow the president of the ceremonies to be present at the gladiatorial show in honour of the deceased which we have already described.

The voyagers next made their way to Oubon, where they arrived in time to witness the coronation of the king. The chief of every village, and the leading men of every province, and indeed all the inhabitants, had been invited to "assist" in the ceremony. On the morning of the appointed day, the strangers were deafened by an uproar of drums and gongs and other unmusical instruments. The noisy orchestra surrounded the palace ; while the royal procession wound through the streets of Oubon, and defiled into its square or market-place. Mounted upon an elephant of great size, which was armed with a pair of formidable tusks, the king made his appearance, encircled by guards on foot and on horseback, and attended by his great dignitaries mounted like himself. A train of smaller elephants followed, carrying the court ladies. The *cortége* finally directed its course to some spacious pavilions erected for the purpose, where the bonzes of the royal pagoda were offering up their prayers.

A few minutes passed, and another tableau was presented. The king was seen enthroned in the largest pavilion. He arose, and, escorted by his principal officers, advanced into the middle of a wide platform, where the bonzes, still uttering their prayers, gathered about him. He threw off his clothes, replacing them by a mantle of white cloth. Then the bonzes drew apart, so as to open up a passage for him ; and he proceeded to place himself, with his body bent into a curve, immediately underneath the sacred dragon. Prayers were recommenced, and the king received the anointing or consecrating *douche;* while a dignitary who stood at one corner of the dais set free a couple of turtle-doves, as a sign that all creation, down even to the animals, should be happy on so auspicious a day.

When the water which was contained in the dragon's body had completely douched the royal person, new garments were brought, over which was thrown a large white robe; and he returned to his place in the centre of the hall. A grand banquet of rice, and cucumbers, and eggs, and pork, and delicious bananas, washed down by copious draughts of rice-wine, concluded the day's proceedings; and in the evening the town was lighted up with fireworks, while bands of singers and musicians traversed the streets.

Lieutenant Garnier, after a brief rest, resumed his exploration of the Mekong, passing through scenery which previously no European had visited. At night he and his companions halted at the most convenient spot, lighted a fire, cooked their meal of rice, and took their rest under the curtain of a starry sky, or beneath such shelter as they could hastily run up. Fatigue assisted them to a speedy slumber; yet their repose was often disturbed by

the cries of the wild elephants which, in large numbers, roamed among the hills on the other side of the
river, or by the roar of some tiger prowling along
the bank. During the day their attention was
sometimes diverted from the contemplation of the
strange and picturesque scenery which surrounded
them, by the necessity of piloting their boat through
the rapids and whirlpools that obstruct the navigation of the river.

In this way they proceeded to Kemarat and Pen-
nom ; and, across an immense plain, remarkable for
its fertility, followed the course of the river, which
runs due north and south, broadening into a lake
of such dimensions that its boundaries cannot be
detected by the naked eye. One morning, as the
mists cleared off, they were surprised at the appearance, on the northern horizon, of dim azure forms,
resembling the deception of the mirage, or clouds of
fantastic outline, or rather a mass of medieval ruins,
with lofty towers and pinnacles, and shattered ramparts. The natives informed them that these were
the mountains of Lakon, at the foot of which they
would arrive on the following day. They found it
difficult to believe in the existence of such mountains, the configuration of which grew stranger and

more fantastic as they drew nearer to them; sometimes exhibiting sheer precipitous declivities, sometimes overhanging masses, while sometimes each summit appeared cloven into deep and shadowy chasms. These enormous rocks of marble of different tints have been heaped up in awful confusion by some convulsion of the terrestrial crust; and forced, by an inconceivable subterranean effort, through the sandstone formation which underlies the superficial strata of the country.

Round the projecting angle of the mountain-mass the river lightly sweeps; and then its broad waters reflect the huts and pagodas of the important town of Lakon. The bank was lined with the barks of traders and fishers; ample nets, suspended to rows of bamboos, dried in the open air. Sheds erected for the convenience of voyagers, piles of wood and merchandise, and loaded rafts, gave an air of animation and activity to the approaches to the town. Our voyagers, well pleased to regain the society of their kind, made haste to unload their boats, while native porters carried their luggage to the house set apart for their accommodation : it stood on the margin of the river, overshadowed by the branches of a huge mango-tree. Here, as soon as the work was done, they stretched themselves on the floor, postponing until the morrow their exploration of the town.

At daybreak they were aroused by the noisy gong of a neighbouring pagoda. Already the river-bank and the town showed signs of life and movement. Curious faces were gathered round the strangers' hut. A large bag of rice, fruit, fish, and some buffalo-steaks dried in the sun, arrived, sent by the mandarin provisionally intrusted with the charge of supplying their wants. The fresh genial morning tempted them forth, and they went from end to end of the town, which seemed both wealthy and populous. The pagodas were numerous, the huts well-constructed, the gardens green and admirably kept. The inhabitants appeared free and happy. Behind the town, in an open space on the border of the rice-fields, some bands of travellers lay encamped under roofs of interwoven foliage. The principal street, which ran along the river-bank, was shaded everywhere by the trees and creepers of the gay gardens that skirted its entire course. It made a pleasant promenade, as through each opening in the rich glossy foliage could be seen the white sands of the shore, the calm crystal river, the forest thickly crowding the opposite bank, and, beyond, the long line of the marble mountains.

After this excursion, our voyagers returned to their hut, which they found an object of attraction to all the curiosity-mongers of Lakon. The most distinguished ladies of the town had assembled to see the strangers, and offer in exchange for European ornaments their richest fruits and freshest vegetables. If Garnier and his companions were surprised at their appearance, they were still more surprised to find in the crowd a group of twenty Annamites, who had emigrated from the French colony of Cochin-China, and had been established at Lakon for some years. As Garnier's escort was also composed of Annamites, the scene between the compatriots thus singularly brought together was one of unbounded ecstasy. Garnier went on a visit to the little Annamite settlement, which repeated in every detail the villages of Cochin-China. In each hut was to be seen the tiny domestic altar, with its lights, and incense, and small statue of Buddha, and broad bands of red paper, inscribed with Chinese characters and symbolical designs. There, too, were the large central table, a mother-of-pearl *plateau*, a complete " tea-equipage" (to use the late Lord Lyt-

ANNAMITES AT LAKON.

ton's phrase), and a bed surrounded by mosquito-
curtains. And no less conspicuous was that want of
cleanliness, both in dwelling and person, which char-
acterize the natives of Cochin-China.

We cannot describe all the objects of interest at
Lakon, or all the excursions which Garnier made in
its neighbourhood. The geologist and botanist of
the expedition adventured a visit to the Marble
Mountains. With a guide and a couple of elephants,
they crossed the river, plunged into the forest-depths,
and found their way to the quarries, where blocks
of marble are excavated for the purpose of being
made into lime of a dazzling whiteness. Then they
penetrated into the grottoes and caverns with which
the mountains abound. As they advanced, the
scenery became more and more picturesque, and
more and more savage : high rugged peaks rose
above the forest trees ; bushes and lianas and para-
sitical plants decked with festoons every rocky projection ; here yawned a gloomy chasm, there towered
aloft a mighty and awful precipice. But the scene
of scenes burst upon them after they had threaded
a gloomy maze of trees and intertangled bamboos.
Two immense walls of sombre rock, several hundred
yards in height, enclosed a broad ravine, which, at

the further extremity, opened on a bare and·shining plain.   On the left, the wall extended to a great distance, forming a long line, decreasing in elevation through the natural effect of the perspective.   That on the right towered above a pile of enormous rocks, heaped together in the wildest confusion ; it seemed to turn like the enceinte of a strong fortification, and was terminated abruptly by a vertical line, broken by numerous gaps.   Between these lofty barriers lay a barren plain ; afar, some miniature pools glittered with a magical effect in the " pale moonlight."   The prospect was closed in the distance by the steep declivities of lofty mountains, surrounding and shutting up, as it were, this gigantic " cirque " or amphitheatre.   About three hundred yards from the entrance rose two vertical rocks, like a couple of slender spires, or rather like two enormous tapers—rose to a prodigious height, isolated, and emerging from a clump of luxuriant verdure which flourished at their feet.   One of these rocks was fully nine hundred feet in elevation.   The other was not so lofty, and seemed to have partially fallen, the ground being everywhere strewn with its wreck.

From this remarkable spectacle the French *savants* proceeded to inspect a superb grotto excavated in the

NATURAL PILLAR IN THE MOUNTAINS OF LAKON.

great wall of cliff, near the two pillar-like masses.
By climbing some rocks they obtained an entry into
it, and found it to form a spacious hall, varying
from forty to eighty feet in height, of great depth,
with a rounded, vaulted roof. The ground was
thick with stalagmites; while stalactites of the most
various shapes depended from the vault, and glittered, like so many mirrors, in the light of torches.

A day or two afterwards, Garnier and his friends,
in returning from a walk in the environs of Lakon,
encountered some Laotians carrying vessels of bamboo, filled with a liquid which at first they supposed
to be water. On tasting it, however, they discovered that it was the wine of the country; sweet-
flavoured, and by no means disagreeable to the
palate; not unlike, indeed, the product of some of
the Rhenish vineyards. It was palm-wine, freshly
made; and to enjoy its *bouquet* and full flavour it
should be drunk in this condition, for it will not
keep more than four-and-twenty hours without fer-
mentation. The Laotians offered to conduct the
strangers to a neighbouring plantation, where they
might observe the different processes of its manufacture. The offer was accepted, and the party soon

arrived at a clearing which was thickly planted
with great borassus palms.   To collect the wine,—
which is, in fact, the sap of the tree,—nothing more
is necessary than to make an incision in the middle
of the head of the tree, at the point where the leaves
branch off, and suspend beneath a bamboo, into which
the sap falls, drop by drop.   In order to reach the
summit of these huge palms, which are straight and
smooth as the main-mast of a ship, the Laotians have
invented a simple and ingenious process.   They
transform the palm into a veritable ladder, by attach-
ing to the trunk, with small strips of flexible ratan,
projecting laths of bamboo, which, jutting out to
right and left at intervals of twelve to fourteen
inches, form so many "rungs," and enable the ascent
of the tree to be rapidly and easily accomplished.

But we must no longer tarry at Lakon.   We
must once more launch the boats of our adventurous
voyagers, and continue our exploration of the great
river.   It waters a populous country, and large
towns are of frequent occurrence on its banks.   We
pass Houton, with its pagodas, its mountains, and
green woods; Saniabury, with its rude pottery-
manufacture; verdurous islands and shining sand-

TAPPING THE BORASSUS PALM.

banks; and the mouths of the many streams which help to swell the abundant volume of the Mekong. From Saniabury the French expedition proceeded to Bouncang, a large and beautiful village at the mouth of the Nam San; thence to Nong Kay, where a Buddhist tat or pyramidal landmark, erected to indicate a sacred spot, or to enshrine a relic, has been washed away from the shore, and now lies half submerged, like a wrecked ship; and thence to Vien Chan, where the river widens into a channel of a thousand yards in width, before it enters the mountain region. Vien Chan, now a heap of ruins, was the former metropolis of the kingdom of Laos; and relics of antiquity spread over a considerable area testify to its ancient prosperity and splendour. The remains of the royal palace are interesting. It does not seem to have been built of very durable materials, the walls and staircases being faced with, and the pavement and flooring composed of, bricks, wood, or a kind of cement; but the entire structure still exhibits a certain elegance of character, and a remarkable wealth of decoration—the columns of wood have been tastefully carved and profusely gilded; and the whole is embellished with mouldings, and arabesques, and fantastic animal-figures.

The absolute silence reigning within the precincts
of a city formerly so rich and populous, was, however, much more impressive than any of its monuments; more impressive even than the deserted
topes or Buddhist temples which raised their domes
in the shadow of the surrounding forest.

These, abandoned by their priests, and constructed of the same materials as the palace, are
rapidly decaying. The rapid vegetation of the
tropics, which softens happily the pitiful aspect of
Desolation with its flowers and verdure, lends to these
ruined sanctuaries, at a distance, a delusive air of
age; tall grasses grow everywhere about the sacred
precincts, creepers and parasites twine round each
column, and vigorous trees force their crests through
the shattered roofs in search of light.

The most considerable temple is Wat Pha Keo,
the royal pagoda. Its timber façade, delicately
wrought, and sparkling with those plates of glass
which the Laotians and the Siamese cunningly
mingle with their gilding in order to produce a
greater effect of brilliancy, shines forth in the midst
of the forest, gracefully framed with blooming lianas,
and profusely garlanded with foliage. Gold has
been unsparingly lavished on the sides of the square

BUDDHIST TAT AT NONG KAY

columns which supported the half-shattered roof;
and a Byzantine style of decoration, very remarkable in effect, has at one time covered every inch of
space. Though this mode of ornamentation is by
no means lasting, it is very charming; and the
numerous pagodas in Vien Chan thus embellished
produced, at a distance, a wonderful impression of
dazzling magnificence.

To the north, in the midst of the forest, is situated a smaller pagoda, which has undergone but
little dilapidation,—that of Wat Sisaket. In its
interior a number of small statues of Buddha are
enshrined in gilded niches, which cover the wall
from floor to ceiling, rivalling the terraces of Boro
Bodor, the celebrated Buddhist monument of Java.
Before the altar was elevated a candelabrum, remarkable for its originality of design and exquisite finish
of workmanship. A few paces distant from the
pagoda was situated the library, an indispensable
appendage of all the temples of Laos; it was partly
destroyed. As no native was near, the French
explorers clambered up the worm-eaten pillars which
supported and isolated from the soil the flooring of
this literary tabernacle: in the interior some sacred
books were scattered about; they were composed of

long narrow strips cut from the leaves of a particular
species of palm, gilded on the edges, and stitched
together in books. Each contained seven or eight
lines of that rounded writing peculiar to the peoples
of the Indo-Chinese peninsula; which differs, as is
recognized at the first glance, from the writing of
India properly so-called, though derived from it.
Finally, attached directly to the pagoda, the
travellers found a rectangular gallery, opening
internally on a court,—its walls covered, like those
of the temple itself, with small niches containing
Buddha statues. This was the vihara (*chon-khon*
in Laotian), or monastery, which served as the residence of the priests ministering in Wat Sisaket.

Some miles above Vien Chan, the Mekong enters
a narrow valley, which is sharply defined and enclosed by two ranges of high hills. Its waters, hitherto
majestic and tranquil, which had peacefully unfolded
silver coil after coil over the vast plateau of central
Laos, now accelerated their course, and tumbled and
eddied among the rocks, ever restless and ever noisy.
The noble river, which had previously measured its
breadth by thousands of yards, now shut up within
two barriers of constantly-increasing elevation, was

MONASTERY OF WAT SISAKET.

now contained in a channel which rarely attained
to five or six hundred yards in width, and from
which it was no more to escape. In dry seasons it
occupied only a small portion of this space, and it
had presented a rugged and broken surface of rock ;
a grand mosaic, where fragments mingled of all
the metamorphic formations,—marbles, schists, ser-
pentines, even jades,—curiously coloured, and sometimes admirably polished.

As the travellers advanced the river grew nar-
rower, and, with a width of three hundred yards
and a depth of twenty-five fathoms, flowed through
a wild and wooded valley, uninhabited except by
the animals of the forest. They passed the mouth
of the Nam Thon; after which they came upon a
dangerous series of rapids, where the foaming waters,
hurled and driven from side to side, and swung
round projecting rocks, and driven against the foot of
precipitous banks, rushed downwards tumultuously,
with all the clang and clash of billows breaking
against a reef. To thread this water-labyrinth, it
was necessary to obtain the assistance of a pilot
from a neighbouring village; and even he was unwilling to promise that the boats of the expedition,
light and small as they were, could be carried up to

the next Muong, that of Xieng Cang. The boats, however, were unloaded, and the stores transferred to the shoulders of sturdy natives, who bore them along the rocks; while others towed the boats with many a lusty pull through the whirl and foam of the rapids. But so laborious and so difficult was the task, that two whole days were spent in effecting the passage of a few miles.

At length they reached Xieng Cang, or, as it is also called, Muong Mai, the "new Muong," which is one of the most important centres of population on the left bank of the Mekong. The river here broadens considerably, and its waters are as peaceful as those of a woodland pool. Opposite to the town rises a beautiful chain of green mountains, in a series of gently-sloping terraces; and these are intersected by delightful Eden-valleys, finely wooded, enamelled with flowers, and brightened by the silver thread of a little brook. The village, or town, is well built; the houses are very lofty; and the inhabitants are employed, according to the season, in the manufacture of cotton and the cultivation of rice. The principal pagoda, situated on the threshold of the rice-fields, near a grove of graceful corypha palms, is richly ornamented in the interior, and, among

PASSAGE OF A RAPID.

other curiosities, contains an ancient carved *porte-cierges* of wood. At the time of Garnier's visit, some Birman traders had displayed the contents of their packs on the steps of the temple, and were selling to the natives their bright-coloured cotton stuffs and English hardware. A road having been made westward from Hoûten, Muong Mai is only a hundred leagues from Moulmein, which lies in nearly the same latitude, and is, as the reader knows, an English colony, and a busy commercial port, at the mouth of the Saluen. From this point spread over the interior of Laos the Peguans, or Birmans of the British possessions, whose knowledge of the wares most readily purchased by European merchants, and the high price at which they sell to the natives their English goods, enable them to accumulate considerable wealth.

Resuming their northward route, and bent upon tracing the river up to its mountain-source, they passed through a fertile and picturesque country, which has been made known to the Western nations by the enterprise of the traveller Mouhot. Leaving behind them the mouth of the Nam Lim, and diverging somewhat to the west, then again to the

north, the voyagers arrived in the neighbourhood of
Pak Lay, where they fell in with a M. Duyshart,
a Hollander in the service of the king of Siam,
and employed by him in a series of geographical
researches, who was descending the river to Bangkok.
They exchanged scientific notes, and it appeared
that Duyshart had surveyed the course of the Cambodia or Mekong for one hundred and twenty miles
above Luang Prabang.

A few hours after this interesting rencontre, the
French expedition crossed the boundary-line of the
kingdom of Luang Prabang, and reached the extremity
of the great rapid of Keng Sao.   Successfully steering their course through its rocks and islets, they
arrived at Pak Lay, a romantically-situated village,
buried in the deep shadows of the primeval forest.
To the north of the village, and almost hidden by
the trees, is situated a small pagoda, entirely deficient
in the accessory buildings which usually surround
a temple at Laos, but better placed for the purpose
of assisting the self-absorption of its priests and
votaries.

As the voyagers proceeded up the river, they
now began to notice a gradual change in the char-

RICE-FIELD AND PAGODA AT MUONG MAI.

acter alike of the inhabitants and the vegetation.
The calcareous mountains which dominated over the
river-valley assumed the most irregular and fantastic forms, and forced it into a constant succession
of broken curves and sharp angular turns. At
times a mass of marble suddenly projected its high
precipitous cliffs, which the river bathed with waters
sometimes foaming, sometimes tranquil.

The Mekong was not at its full height at the
time our voyagers ascended it: a great part of its
bed lay bare; and a person, on landing, before he
could reach the bank had to traverse wide spans
rugged with rocks. Here and there spread immense
sandbanks, on which were erected large fishing-
stations—veritable towns of bamboo—already abandoned by the fishermen in anticipation of the quick-
coming rise of the waters.

For three days the expedition continued its course.
Not a single hut was visible anywhere. The only
incidents of their voyage were the rapids, which
occurred at intervals of three or four miles. These,
for the most part, were formed by the shingle and
rocks accumulated at their mouth by the numerous
streamlets which the river here receives. By dint
of vigorous exertions, the native boatmen "poled"

their light barks through each swift current. At
times the scene was illuminated by the arrowy
flashes of a storm-swept sky; and peals of thunder,
resounding among the mountains in multitudinous
reverberations, mingled with the roar of the waters.
Hail frequently fell in heavy showers during these
gales, which lasted usually about half an hour, and
abruptly lowered the temperature four or five
degrees.

The river's course was remarkably direct, and lay
almost due north. At certain points it completely
filled its bed ; its breadth was then reduced to about
one hundred and fifty yards ; and the hills which
bordered it were of so regular an appearance that
the stream assumed all the features of an artificial
canal. A series of miniature cascades flashed their
silver spray in all directions, as they descended the
verdurous slopes.

Luang Prabang, at which our voyagers in due
course arrived, is the modern capital of Laos. It is
picturesque and pleasant to the view, and enjoys the
advantage of a favourable situation. Its houses are
very numerous, and are arranged in parallel lines
around a small central hillock, which, like a dome

PAGODA AT PAK LAY.

of verdure, rises above the mass of gray thatched
roofs. On the summit a tat or dagoba elevates its
sharp arrowy pinnacle above a belt of trees, so as to
form a landmark for all the surrounding country.
Upon the terraced declivities of this quasi-sacred
eminence are situated several pagodas, the red roofs
of which are vividly defined against the sombre
green vegetation. At the foot of the cliffs, which
are about fifty feet high, stretches a row of perma-
nent rafts, on which numerous huts are erected, com-
posing beneath the town a kind of second town or
river-suburb, connected with the capital itself by
zigzag paths, shining like white ribbons in the distance. Hundreds of boats of all sizes move rapidly
along this floating city; while large and heavy rafts,
coming down from the upper waters of the river,
seek a convenient nook for mooring and unloading
their cargoes. At the foot of the cliffs a crowd of
boatmen and porters hurry to and fro; and the hum
of voices mingles confusedly with the murmur of
the stream, and the whisper of the palm-trees which
wave their feathery crests upon its smiling and fertile banks.

After a brief sojourn at this interesting and lively
city, the French voyagers, animated by their desire

to open up a new channel of commercial enterprise,
and discover a practicable route from Cambodia to
China, resumed their ascent of the Mekong.   They
found that, above Luang Prabang, it narrowed considerably, and resumed its wild and romantic aspect.
The mountains on either hand exhibited a succession
of bold, dark, cloven crests; their lowest terraces,
impending over the river-banks, being frequently
ornamented by a pyramid, the tomb of a pious bonze
or the shrine of an imaginary relic, the slender form
of which harmonized well with the character of the
landscape.

Passing the confluence of the Nam Hou, they
came upon the cavern of Pak Hou, which the Buddhist priests have covered with religious decoration,
and adorned with the gifts of munificent pilgrims.
Thence they proceeded to Ban Tanoun; and from
Ban Tanoun to Xieng Khong, the second in importance of the towns of the great province of
Muong Nan.   There they experienced some difficulty
in obtaining permission to enter the Burmese territory;   and, moreover, they found that they had
nearly reached the limit of the navigable portion of
the river.   Few are the obstacles, however, which
cannot be conquered by resolution and energy; and

BAMBOO BRIDGE AT XIENG KHONG

on the 14th of June the expedition left Xieng Khong
in six light boats, drawing but little water, and
continued the ascent of the river, which here bends
to the westward, and flows across an apparently
boundless plain. It is crossed near the town or
village by a graceful but slender bridge of bamboo,
from which may be obtained a charming view of its
graceful sweep through a luxuriance of tropical vegetation.

At Muong Lim the expedition were compelled to
abandon their boats. Its members found themselves
there in the midst of a population differing in race
from any they had previously met with. They
seem, these Mou-tsen, to be of Caucasian origin.
Their costume is very complicated, and even taste-
ful; and the tinsel and embroidery with which they
cover their persons gives them a certain resemblance
to the inhabitants of some parts of Brittany. The
head-gear of the women has, at all events, the merit
of originality. It consists of a series of rings of
bamboo, covered with plaited straw, and fastened on
the top of the head. The brim of this kind of hat
is enriched over the forehead with silver balls; above
are two rows of pearl-white glass beads; on the left

side depends a tuft of white and red cotton thread, from which issues a loop formed of strings of many-coloured pearls. This coiffure, which is capable of infinite modifications, is completed with an abundance of leaves and flowers. The women also wear a tight-fitting bodice, the sleeves and edges of which are trimmed with pearls, and a short petticoat reaching to the knee. The legs are wrapped round with leggings, which begin at the ankle, and cover the whole of the calf. These leggings, too, are ornamented with a row of pearls about half-way up. The toilette is completed by ear-rings of coloured beads or balls of blown silver, bracelets, belts, collars, and shoulder-belts crossed over the bosom. As for the men, they wear the usual turban, loose short pantaloons, and a waistcoat with silver buttons. With both sexes a necessary addition to the attire is a kind of cloak or mantle of leaves, in shape like a book half-open, which is fastened to the neck, and in rainy weather is brought up over the head like a loose cover. The women, when carrying burdens, add to their already complex costume a wooden board across the shoulders, so made as to fit into the neck ; and to this is suspended the basket containing the load. In front the board is kept in its

FOREST ROAD NEAR MUONG LIM.

place by cords, which are attached to the waist-belt
or held in the hand.

Having obtained the necessary authorization to
push their researches further, the adventurers set
out from Muong Lim on the 1st of July, with an
escort of natives carrying their instruments, provisions, and stores. At Puleo, finding the demands of
the porters more than their limited funds could
afford to meet, they reduced their baggage to the
smallest possible proportions, and were thus enabled
to dispense with the services of some of their attendants. They found the banks of the Cambodia frequented by numerous caimans, whose eggs are collected and eaten by the inhabitants. By day the
journey was rendered pleasant through the constant
succession of novel scenes. They made their way
over a hilly and richly-wooded country, occasionally
coming upon cotton plantations of exceeding richness ; at other times upon delicious rills of crystal
which spread their silver network over a fresh green
expanse of flower-enamelled sward. Then they
crossed a stretch of fertile rice-fields ; and again they
plunged into fresh glades, where a path wound in
and out of clumps of palms and tropical trees, and

waving ferns and rare flowering shrubs grew in
luxuriant masses.   But sometimes, at night, their
experience was rather painful.   They generally constructed a rude shelter of boughs and interwoven
leaves ; but this was often insufficient to protect
them against the heavy rains that fell during passing
storms, and was useless, of course, as a defence
against the legions of leeches and mosquitoes which
haunted the forest-depths.

After leaving a place called Siem-lap, they arrived
on the borders of a half-dried torrent, the rocky bed
of which was strangely bare of vegetation.   The
stones, among which a thin thread of water found
its way, wore a curious appearance ; they were white,
and covered with saline incrustations.   The travellers tasted the water ; it was warm.   The three or
four sources of this singular stream rose, a short
distance off, at the foot of a wall of rocks : as they
escaped among the shingle they exhaled a cloud
of vapour, and their temperature was shown by the
thermometer to be not less than 154° F.

Through a beautiful ravine they made their way
to the picturesque village of Sop Yong.   The richest
and most magnificent vegetation imaginable grew
close to the very edge of the river, and the travellers

were frequently compelled to take to its waters, swollen as they were by the constant rains, and breast as best they could the violence of the current. The next stage after Sop Yong was Ban Passang, which is described as an agglomeration of villages situated on a fertile table-land, in the heart of a rice-growing district. It is situated in the territory of Muong Yong, the chief town lying further to the westward. For Muong Yong the travellers set out on the 7th of August. They traversed a plain abundantly watered by streams which all flow into the Nam Yong, a branch of the great river. Over the chief of these little tributaries, the Nam Ouang, is thrown a wooden bridge; and this agreeable accommodation, a very great rarity in the land of the Laotians, pleasantly surprised our gallant explorers; they looked upon it as the sign of a more advanced civilization, which before long would exhibit itself more completely. A considerable portion of the plain was laid out in rice-fields; the rest was all swamp and morass. They passed by several villages which wore an unusual aspect of ease and comfort. Pagodas with curved roofs attracted the eye, and bore witness to the influence of Chinese architecture and the vicinity of the Celestial Empire.

At Muong Yong the expedition was delayed until the 8th of September, owing to the difficulty of obtaining the permission of the king of Birmah to cross those Laotian territories which are now included within the borders of his extensive dominions. The interval was occupied in short excursions in the neighbourhood, and in studying the manners and customs of the inhabitants. It was with no small pleasure, however, that the French adventurers took their departure, and continued their bold advance into regions of which European geographers knew but little. Their route led them to the important town of Muong You, where they paid visits of courtesy to the principal mandarins, the Burman representative, and the king of Muong You himself. This prince received them with dignified hospitality, and entertained them at a banquet, which was "served up" in magnificent style, and with a dazzling display of gold and silver plate. He is described as a young man of twenty-six, with a graceful figure and handsome countenance. He was attired in a dress of green satin, embroidered with red flowers; and the fire of the rubies which hung pendent from his ears illuminated the silken reflections of his rich costume. He was seated on

TRAVELLING IN A RAVINE NEAR SOP YONG

cushions glittering with gold tracery. Around him were ranged in respectful attitudes the mandarins of the palace; at his feet, the sword and vessels of gold, finely wrought, which are the symbol of royalty.

From Muong You the expedition struck across a romantic country—as yet provided with but few facilities for travellers—to Xieng Hong, where new impediments were thrown in the way of their further progress. Having obtained admission to the presence of the king, they succeeded, however, in obtaining the royal favour, and made their way along the valley of the Nam Yong, which is bounded on either hand by lofty mountains, to Muong La, or, as it is also called, Se-mao, situated on the frontier of China; that mysterious land which has preserved its own strange civilization intact for upwards of two thousand years, and still offers a sullen resistance to the progressive influences of the West.

Once upon Chinese territory, they found their march comparatively easy. Order reigned everywhere; and in all directions could be seen the evidences of a constant and energetic industry. At Pou-eul, a village of salt-pits, with its smoke, its dusky houses, its hoarse sounds of active life, our travellers felt that they were once more in the midst of a thriving civilization, and could almost have believed that they were located in a small industrial town of Europe. Numerous convoys of asses, mules, oxen, and horses ascended and descended the long sloping street along which were erected the different factories, carrying thither wood and charcoal and cordage, and carrying away salt. Above the village rose a pagoda, crowning the summit of a hill so high that the murmur of the life below could not reach it. Groves of pines stretched far away on either hand; and along the declivities were ranged abundant rice-fields, situated one above the other in symmetrical terraces.

The expedition had now left the valley of the Mekong, and were wholly uncertain whether the route prescribed for them by the Chinese authorities would bring them again in contact with the great Cambodian river. We propose, however, to follow M. Garnier, as his wanderings led him through a country hitherto unknown to Europeans.

In the early part of November our adventurers struck the right bank of the Pa-pien-kiang of the Chinese, which is apparently identical with the

INTERVIEW WITH THE KING OF MUONG YOU.

Nam-La, an affluent of the Mekong. Thence they ascended into the table-land of Yunnan, rendered familiar to English ears in connection with the enterprise and murder of Mr. Margary; and reached Tong-kuan, or "the Fortress of the East,"—a strongly-built town, with a large garrison, posted on a commanding ridge between two river-valleys. Afterwards they crossed another considerable stream, the Poukou-kiang, and continued their march through valleys and over hills where the industry of man has softened the wilder features of the scenery, and made the wilderness to blossom like a garden. In a few days they made their appearance at Yuen-kiang, where they seem to have been welcomed with almost royal honours. The town is large and populous, with every indication of commercial activity and wealth. It has several handsome pagodas, which have something of the Buddhist type about them. The markets are well supplied with provisions of excellent quality and low price. Oranges are almost "given away;" and potatoes are so cheap and plentiful that an Irish peasant would think himself in an earthly paradise. The country around the town is highly cultivated; cotton being largely grown, and mulberry-trees for

the silkworm nurseries. A rich and radiant plain
is watered by the stream of the Ho-ti-kiang, which,
opposite the town, measures about one-fifth of a mile
in breadth.

At Pou-pio M. Garnier hired a light canoe, and,
in company with some trading barks, began the
descent of the Ho-ti-kiang, which for some distance
swirled in a narrow channel between mountain-
walls of two thousand five hundred to. three thousand feet in height. Each torrent which rent these
rocky barriers brought down with it an immense
quantity of stones and pebbles, that encumbered
the river-bed with shoals and banks, and pent up
the waters in foaming rapids. M. Garnier was
bound for Lin-ngan, but these numerous obstacles
greatly impeded his progress. But by degrees
the river-bed broadened, the heights receded on
either hand, and the stream flowed with a full
and tranquil current through a gently undulating
country, well cultivated, and studded with populous
villages.

In due time he reached Lin-ngan, where, as the
first European who had visited it, he became an
object of special attraction. An inspection of the
town showed him that it was neatly and regularly

MOUNTAIN VILLAGE AND RICE-FIELDS NEAR POU-EUL

built, and of rectangular form, measuring about two thousand yards in length, by one thousand in breadth. In the centre were gardens and pagodas decorated with much taste; and a large and fully-stocked market was a scene of very picturesque animation.

CHAPTER II.

THE attentions which a curious populace lavish upon a stranger are apt to become a trouble and a burden, as Garnier experienced, when, after an interesting survey of the environs of Lin-ngan, he returned to the town. His steps were closely dogged by crowds of idlers and sightseers. On his arrival at the pagoda where lodging had been provided for him, behold! the balconies, the towers, the very roofs, were thronged with wondering eyes.

As he entered the court, the multitude pressed in upon him, and hemmed him up at last in a narrow space, where they evidently designed to hold him fast until their curiosity was satiated. Angry and ashamed, he bore their scrutiny for an hour; when, his strength and patience giving way, he made a sudden exit into his lodgings, closing the door of the court behind him. It proved, however, an insufficient barrier against the surging throng. They broke through it in a second, and were with difficulty kept back a little by Garnier's small escort of soldiers, who had attended him from Yuen-kiang. The lieutenant succeeded at last in closing the door. Then loud and long were the reproaches which the rearmost ranks heaped on those in front for having recoiled before a barbarian from the West!

A stone, hurled through the grating, struck Garnier full in the face; others followed, until there seemed every likelihood of his undergoing the tortures of the ancient punishment by lapidation! Yet he yielded not an inch, but leaning against the door, which shook before the storm of missiles, seized his revolver, and fired it in the air. Firearms of such deadly powers are not known at Lin-ngan, and the crowd, in the firm belief that by discharging his weapon Garnier had virtually disarmed himself, recommenced their volleys of stones. He fired again, and again, and again; and the people, terrified by a weapon which apparently was inexhaustible, fell back in a panic, and the danger proved to be past.

Soon afterwards Garnier was joined by the rest

of the expedition; and setting out from inhospitable
Lin-ngan, the little company of explorers proceeded
on their way to Yunnan, the capital of a province of
the same name.

Yunnan is a town of some importance, with a
very numerous and industrious population. Every
thoroughfare presents a scene of the liveliest activity.
The town is surrounded by a high and massive wall;
and from the south gate extends a long broad street,
lined with shops, each of which has on its front a
sign in gilded characters, while the interior is filled
with wares of extraordinary richness and variety.
Some Jesuit missionaries are stationed here.

The travellers now entered the green valley of
Kon-tchang, through the leafy shades of which
tumbles a sparkling, noisy stream, while on either
hand rise venerable trees, with trunks bent and
contorted as if by some sudden convulsion. Thence
they ascended to Mong-kou by a difficult road, winding round the precipitous flank of a wind-swept
height, the summit of which, some twelve thousand
feet above the sea, was capped with snow. Wild and
romantic was the character of the scenery, reminding
the travellers of that of Switzerland. At intervals
the expedition met with a check to its progress

VALLEY OF KON-TCHANG.

from the jealousy of the Chinese officials, but resolution and tact overcame every obstacle. Through the broad valley of Tong-chuen they debouched on a small but well-cultivated plain, where the solid embankment of the bed of a torrent formed a kind of causeway, raised seven to ten feet above the surrounding level. From the sides of this elevated dyke issue numerous canals, which distribute the fertilizing waters of the stream over all the thirsty fields. Here, as in many other districts of China, the patient industry of the labourer has transformed a devastating force into a fountain of wealth and fecundity. The aspect of the plain is very grateful to the eye. Yellow clusters of the colza mingle with the white or purple corollas of the poppies. From the ridge which terminates it is visible a deep cleft in the barrier of mountains that stretches far along the horizon. This is the valley of the Blue River, locally known as the Kin-cha-kiang, or "River of the Golden Sand."

Our explorers came upon this river on the 31st of January. It rolled its clear deep waters in a ravine two thousand feet below them. Their route, however, still lay along the mountain-sides, and they suffered severely from the rigour of the cold and the heavy

storms of snow which beat continually upon their
devoted heads.   On the 3rd of February they
crossed the most elevated point they had reached in
all their wanderings,—the barometer indicating an
elevation of nearly ten thousand feet.   Then they
began to descend, each stage opening up to their
enraptured gaze a succession of glorious mountain-
views, relieved by occasional glimpses of finely wooded
valleys, and of bright streams that leaped and bounded
in their haste to join the great river of the plains.
As they descended the temperature necessarily grew
warmer, and out of the inclemencies of winter they
rapidly passed into the genial airs of spring.

On the 29th of February, from the summit of the
col which forms the little valley of Kuang-tsa-pin,
they discovered the lake of Taly, one of the finest
and grandest pictures which had excited their
admiration since they entered on their expedition.
The background consists of a lofty chain of snow-
capped mountains, at the foot of which the blue
waters of the lake break up the plain into a maze
of low promontories covered with gardens and
villages.   A short descent brought them to the
borders of the lake, which they passed to the northward in order to reach its eastern shore.   The many

CROSSING A RAVINE.

villages through which they took their way exhibited the cruellest traces of devastation. Only
the cultivated fields seem to have been spared, and
these presented a flourishing appearance. In due
time they arrived before the gates of the fortress of
Hiang-kuan ; which, erected at the very base of the
mountain, and on the margin of the lake, completely
barred the passage. There they learned from the
mandarin in charge, that he would not allow them
to continue their journey, until permission had been
obtained from the sultan of Taly. This reached
them on the following day ; and, on the 2nd of
March, the journey was resumed. They passed
through Hiang-kuan, the walls of which bathe on
the one side their feet in the waters of the lake, and
on the other ascend the flanks of the mountain, which
forms a tremendous precipice, rendering the defile
very easy of defence.

Beyond, the shore of the lake again expanded
into a magnificent plain, in the centre of which is
situated the city of Taly. At the southern extremity of the lake the mountains again close in upon
its waters ; and this second defile is commanded by
another fortress—that of Hia-kuan. Hia-kuan and
Hiang-kuan, surrounded by massive crenelated ram -

parts, are the two gates of Taly. Defended by brave men they would be impregnable, and render access to the city impossible except by water.

A great paved causeway crosses the plain of Hiang-kuan to Taly. Escorted by ten soldiers, the French travellers entered the latter city by its north gate. In a few moments an immense crowd gathered in their rear, and lined each side of the great street which traverses Taly from north to south. Having arrived in front of the sultan's palace—a crenelated building of sombre and severe aspect—they halted to parley with a couple of mandarins who had been sent to meet them. During this vexatious pause they were surrounded and pressed upon by the crowd, and a soldier violently snatched off the hat of one of the strangers—probably in order that the sultan, who was regarding them from an upper balcony, might the better see his face. This insolence was punished immediately by a blow which drew blood from the aggressor's countenance, and gave rise to an indescribable tumult. The interposition of the two mandarins, the resolute attitude of the Annamites, who grouped themselves around the French travellers, and unsheathed their sword-bayonets, arrested, however, the hostile demonstrations of the crowd, and they reached without further *contretemps* the yamen assigned to them for a residence, situated at the southern extremity of the town.

Immediately after their arrival, a mandarin of higher rank than any they had previously seen presented himself as the formal representative of the sultan, and asked who they were, whence they came, and what they wanted.

Through the medium of one Père Leguilcher, a Jesuit missionary, who had accompanied them, Garnier replied, that they had been sent by the French Government to explore the countries watered by the Lan-tsan-kiang; that having arrived in Yunnan some months ago, they had learned that a new kingdom had been established at Taly, and had desired to pay their respects to its ruler, with the view of opening up commercial and friendly relations between France and him. Some explanations of the scientific object and really pacific character of their mission were added. Garnier offered an excuse also for having only presents of small value to offer to the sultan ; and for being unable, along with the officers of the expedition, to appear before him in suitable costume, the length and difficulties of their journey having compelled them to leave behind almost all the baggage. The mandarin replied very graciously that there was no need for apologies on that score, and that as they were, they would be welcome. To prevent mistakes, Garnier then asked for details as to the ceremonial observed at an audience of the sovereign. It was customary, said the mandarin, to make three genuflexions before the sultan. On Garnier objecting to this servile homage, he consented to allow the French usage, with the condition that no one carried arms into the august presence. After an interchange of compliments, the mandarin took his leave, while the Frenchmen remained enraptured with his cordiality and straightforwardness.

Before long he returned, accompanied by a ta-seu —that is, by one of the eight great dignitaries who compose the council of the sultan. Both requested Lieutenant Garnier to repeat the explanations he had previously given as to the objects of the expedition; and he did so, in the fewest words possible. "You were not, then, sent expressly by your sovereign to Taly?" "How could that be," replied the lieutenant, "when at our departure nobody in France

knew that the town had a king?" They then requested M. Garnier to intrust to them, for the purpose of showing them to the sultan, the Chinese
letters, of which he was the bearer, to the king of
Se-chuen. To this he consented; and they withdrew, apparently quite satisfied.

The first night at Taly was undisturbed. The
lieutenant's intention was, if all went well, to leave
his companions to rest themselves for a few days in
the city; while he and Père Leguilcher pushed forward to the banks of the Lan-tsan-kiang, about
four days' journey, and ascended that river as far as
Li-kiang-foo, where the remainder of the expedition
would rejoin him in due course.

At nine o'clock next morning, when he was col-
lecting all the information necessary for the execution of this project, a messenger came from the sultan
to fetch Père Leguilcher. He did not return until
noon, and then his face was overclouded. The sultan
refused to see them, and had issued orders that they
were to quit the city on the following morning, and
return by the route they came. "Make known to
the strangers," he had said, "that they may seize
all the lands bordering upon the Lan-tsan-kiang,
but they will be compelled to halt on the frontiers

of my kingdom. They may subjugate the eighteen provinces of China; but that which I govern will cause them more trouble than all the rest of the empire. Dost thou not know," he continued, "that it is but three days since I put to death three Malays? If I grant their lives to your companions, it is only because they are strangers, and on account of the letters of recommendation which they carry. But let them hasten their return. They may have sketched my mountains, and fathomed the depths of my rivers; but they will not succeed in conquering them. As for thee," concluded the sultan, in a softer tone, "I know thy religion, and have read its books. Mohammedans and Christians are brothers. Return to thy place of residence, and I will make thee a mandarin, to the end that thou mayst govern thy people."

Throughout the interview, the father was kept standing, and not allowed to speak; overwhelmed with questions to which no reply was permitted, interpellated and hooted at by the crowd.

To what circumstance, says M. Garnier, was so abrupt a change attributable? Undoubtedly to the influence of the military advisers of the king, who would be unable to believe in a purely scientific and

disinterested mission. A despotism sprung from a
revolution, abhorred by the masses whom it overwhelmed with imposts, existing only through terror
and crime, is forced to be cruel and suspicious. The
official relations between the French explorers and
the Chinese authorities had placed the former, with
regard to the sultan of Taly, in a delicate position
which justified his mistrust.

During the rest of the day, the travellers were
visited by a great number of Mohammedan function-
aries, actuated by curiosity or a desire to watch
their doings. They thought it prudent, therefore,
to abstain from sketching or taking notes. About
five o'clock, the sultan sent for the chief of their
escort; who returned soon afterwards, and said that
he had orders to conduct them back to Hiang-kuan
on the following morning. He showed M. Garnier
at the same time a sealed document, which he had
to convey to the mandarin of that fortress. A few
presents attached him to the interests of the French
explorers, who arranged to start with him at daybreak and avoid traversing the town. For Garnier
feared lest, the sultan's suspicions and anger being
known, the crowd should break out into open
hostility, or a few soldiers attempt to satisfy their

ruler's secret desire without actually compromising him.

At nightfall, the lieutenant took care to see that all the weapons of his party were loaded, and instructed them what steps to take in case of a surprise. He sought, by liberal promises, to secure the complete fidelity of the porters.

The night was spent in a painful condition of expectancy. A sentinel had been stationed at their door, who followed them each time they went out. M. Garnier dreaded every moment the arrival of an order to prohibit their departure, and transform their temporary confinement into definite captivity. About eleven o'clock one of the great mandarins of the sultan sent to inquire by what route they intended to return; and received for reply, that they did not know. The night passed without any other incident.

At five in the morning they were on the march, well armed, and carefully grouped; they turned the city of Taly by the south and east, and with scarcely a halt crossed the twenty miles that separated them from Hiang-kuan. As they were about to enter the first gate of the fortress, the chief of their escort stopped them, and said he was ordered, pending the arrival of fresh instructions from the sultan, to lodge them in a small yamen which he obligingly pointed out.

Garnier pretended to regard as a special act of courtesy what was evidently neither more nor less than a disguised sequestration, and replied that, after the cold welcome he had received at Taly, he could not accept the sultan's hospitality. Unwilling, however, that this hurried retreat should look too like a flight, he added that if the mandarin of Hiang-kuan had any communications to make, he would await them in the little wayside *auberge* where he had rested on his way to Taly.

The Mohammedan officer objected that he would be assuming a grave responsibility if he allowed any such modification of the sultan's orders. But Garnier was resolute; having determined, if necessary, to force a passage before he could have time to arouse the garrison of Hiang-kuan. While the sultan's lieutenant put his horse at a gallop to forewarn the governor of the dispute which had arisen, Garnier led his little company through the fortress gates, without encountering any fresh obstacles, and in a few minutes was encamped at the *auberge* already spoken of, with the open country before him.

He had scarcely arrived when the governor of Hiang-kuan sent for Père Leguilcher. He offered him an enormous price for the revolver which Garnier had intended for the sultan, and stated that he had orders to furnish them with a new escort, and two mandarins to accompany them to the frontier, and regulate the stages of their journey; and further, that they were to pass the night at Hiang-kuan, and wait until the following morning for the arrival of the said mandarins and escort.

Garnier replied that he would make a present of the weapon, but that he did not sell arms; that in his journey he reserved to himself full liberty of action, and that he cared nothing at all about the mandarins and the promised escort. This he conclusively showed by starting in the evening for Ma-cha, a village situated at the northern extremity of the lake.

On the 5th of March the journey was continued; and by nightfall the expedition reached the town of Kuang-tia-pin. Their arrival was immediately made known to the commandant of the neighbouring fort, who sent for Père Leguilcher. The good monk was filled with alarm at the thought of the probable

results of the interview. The commandant might
have received orders to separate from their interpreter the little company of strangers; who, left to
themselves, unacquainted with the language and
ignorant of the customs of the country, might the
more easily be entrapped into an ambuscade! On
the other hand, the route lay underneath the guns
of the fort, and it was imprudent to come to an open
rupture with its governor. They contented themselves, therefore, with replying that the evening was
too far advanced for a visit, but that Père Leguilcher would accept the invitation next morning.

This answer did not satisfy; and three soldiers
presented themselves with orders for the father to
follow them.

The poor missionary, overcome with terror, thought
that his last hour had come. It seemed to him as
dangerous to resist as to obey. M. Garnier had to
decide for him; and he repeated to the soldiers the
reply already given, and desired them to be content
with it. They insisted on their instructions with
all the insolence and astonishment inspired by a resistance to which they were unaccustomed. Alarmed
by their threats, which Père Leguilcher understood
much better than his companions, the missionary

wished to comply ; but Garnier detained him, while his Annamite attendants showed the soldiers "the way out." The latter retired, vowing that they would return in great force, and that the heads of the strangers should soon be adorning the posts in the market-place.

By this time the travellers had become accustomed to such "brave words," and gave little heed to them. They took, however, the necessary precautions : each man received a revolver in addition to his carbine, and even Père Leguilcher consented to equip himself with carnal weapons. All the approaches to the *auberge* were guarded, and the utmost vigilance was maintained throughout the night. They were but ten in number ; but as each was equipped with carbine and revolver, they could discharge seventy shots without reloading, which would suffice to keep at a respectful distance a whole regiment of Mohammedans. But no enemy made his appearance.

At daybreak, after having passed in review before them all their porters, and appointed the town of Too-tong-tse as a rendezvous, Garnier and his companions, on horseback, escorted the Jesuit missionary to the gate of the fortress. They then informed the commandant that the father had come to pay the desired visit, but that it could not be prolonged beyond ten minutes; if at the expiration of that time the father had not returned, they would come in quest of him. This peremptory message was intended to produce an impression on people accustomed to see everybody trembling before them. Such language to them would be terrifically novel! It had a good effect. The governor of the fortress contented himself with communicating to Père Leguilcher the order he had received from Taly to escort them to the frontier. The father replied in the words which Garnier had addressed to the governor of Hiang-kuan, and his interlocutor did not insist; he even begged him to shorten the interview, for fear, he said, he should overstay the time allotted, and arouse the impatience of the "great men." And so, an hour later, the whole party arrived in safety at the worthy father's residence, where they enjoyed ten days of entire rest, rendered necessary by the fatigue and emotion they had recently undergone.

On the 7th another messenger arrived from the fort, with a request that Père Leguilcher would come "alone" to consult with the governor on the stages of the travellers' journey. No notice was taken of the communication.

In spite of the rapidity with which M. Garnier had been compelled to pursue his march, he contrived to collect some interesting particulars of the country, its inhabitants, and resources.

The lake of Taly, situated at an elevation above the sea-level of upwards of seven thousand five hundred feet, measures about twenty miles from north to south, with an average breadth of two miles. Its depth is very considerable,—exceeding three hundred and twenty feet at some points. There appear to be several islands scattered towards the south-east. The level of the lake is higher than that of the neighbouring rivers, and its overflow may possibly help to feed those on the north and east, which belong to the Blue River basin. Ostensibly it pours forth its waters at its southern extremity by a river which empties itself into the Mekong. At the mouth of this river, which is not navigable, stands the fortress of Hia-kuan, already spoken of. Shortly after issuing from the lake, it divides into two branches, but these unite again lower down. During the rainy season the waters rise fully seventeen feet; in the dry season, the chain of the Tien Song mountains, on the western shore of the lake, send down a succession of violent squalls, which greatly impede its navigation. This chain, the elevation of which is estimated at sixteen thousand feet, is clothed with snow for nine months in the year. On the opposite bank rises a mass of heights belonging to a range of inferior importance. Between these mountains and the lake some richly-cultivated fields slope gently to the edge of the deep blue waters.

The lake abounds in fish, which are principally caught by birds trained for the purpose. The process adopted is better than that known in Europe as *de pêche au cormoran.*

The fishermen set out at early morn, making a tremendous din and clamour, so as to awaken the attention of the numerous troops of birds slumbering around them. They embark on board flat-bottomed boats, each provided with a well, which they allow to drift along slowly, while one of them, stationed at the bow, throws into the water enormous balls of rice. The fish hasten in immense shoals to enjoy the banquet; and the fishing-birds, flocking round the boats in great numbers, dive and reappear immediately, each with a fish in its bill. As fast as they fill their pouch, the boatmen empty it into the interior of the bark, leaving to each winged fisher just enough to satisfy its appetite and encourage its ardour. In half an hour each boat is loaded, and the boatmen hasten to dispose of their stores at the nearest market.

The plain of Taly formerly contained upwards of one hundred and fifty villages, which the sultan has attempted to repeople almost exclusively with Mohammedans. The eastern shore is inhabited by the Min-kia and Pen-ti populations, who are descended from the first Chinese colonists whom the Mongolian dynasty sent into Yunnan after the conquest of that province. The Min-kia come from the neighbourhood of Nankin. The women do not mutilate their feet; and the young people of both sexes wear a kind of bonnet, of original form, ornamented by a silver pearl. Evidence of their admixture with the former inhabitants of the country is found in their costumes and language. These ancient Chinese emigrants are treated with contempt by pure-blooded Chinese; and hence results an antagonism which not a little contributed to ensure the neutrality of the Min-kia, at the beginning of hos-

tilities between the Mohammedans and the Impe-
rialists. But, after a while, the despotic and violent
acts of the rulers of Taly exasperated even this
pacific race ; and, led by an energetic chief named
Tong, the Min-kia long maintained a successful
resistance against the Mohammedans. Tong fell in
battle in 1866, and the conquerors pursued his
family with merciless vengeance. At present, the
natives of the districts contiguous to Taly, dis-
organized and without a leader, submit to, while
hating, the domination of the sultan. The Pen-ti
occupy more particularly the plain of Tong-chuen,
north of the lake, and the district of the Pe-yen-tsin.
Their costume is original and characteristic.

Under different names, the Lolos, or representa-
tives of the autochthonous race, inhabit the summits
of the mountains, and assert their independence.
With their continual forays they harass the dwellers
in the plains. Certain districts in the vicinity of
Pien-kio pay to one of these tribes, the Tcha-Su, an
annual sum by way of blackmail, in order to secure
their cattle. Even this payment, however, does not
protect them from occasional depredations; and they
cannot claim, when their herds are carried off, more
than half their value.

A considerable trade is carried on between Taly and Tibet, consisting of imports of *kuang-lien*, a bitter root much used in Chinese medicine, woollen stuffs, stag-horns, bear-skins, fox-skins, wax, oils, and resinous gums. Exports from Yunnan include tea, cottons, rice, wine, sugar, mercery, and hardware.

The industrial production of the kingdom of Taly has diminished considerably since the war. Formerly, it was of much importance from a metallurgical point of view. The copper mines of Long-pao, Ta-kong, and Pe-iang are the most valuable in the whole country, where are also found deposits of gold, silver, mercury, iron, lead, and zinc. At Ho-kin paper is made from bamboo. The stems of the plant are made up into bundles of equal length, which are peeled and macerated in lime. They are afterwards placed in an oven, and steamed for twenty days; then they are exposed to a current of cold water, and deposited in layers in a second oven, each layer being covered with a coating of pease-meal and lard. After another "cooking," they are converted into a kind of paste, which is extended on trellis-work in excessively thin layers, and dried in the sun. In this way the manufacturers turn out their sheets of a paper coarse and uneven enough, but very stout.

HE French expedition, finding further progress impossible, resolved at length on retracing its steps to Saigon, and accordingly set out in that direction on the 15th of March. On the 3rd of April it arrived at Tong-chuen, where Lieutenant Garnier heard of the death of his chief, M. de Lagrée. Four days later, the gallant little band, several of its members suffering from fever, resumed its march. On the 9th, M. Garnier crossed the deep swift waters of the Ngieoo-nan in a ferry-boat, which runs on a cable moored from bank to bank. On the 11th he reached Tchao-tong.

Here he and his comrades met with a kindly welcome, and were lodged in the house of a native priest, who had charge of the few Christian inhabitants of the town. The crowd, as usual, displayed an extraordinary amount of curiosity and impor-

tunity.   The *tche-hien*, or administrator of the
Tchao-tong district, paid them a visit immediately
on their arrival, and invited them to dine with him
on the following evening.   The repast included
fourteen courses at the least, to say nothing of the
cucumber-seed, the mandarinas, and the li-tchi, served
up as preliminaries.   There was nothing, however,
peculiarly worthy of the attention of gourmands,
except a dainty dish of pigeons' eggs, and a particular kind of fish, caught in a neighbouring pond,
the flesh of which had a peculiar flavour.   During
the repast, the ladies of the household closely scruti-
nized the features of the strangers through a lattice,
laughing heartily at their awkwardness in using the
Chinese utensils.

Tchao-tong, like all Chinese towns of importance,
is surrounded by a bastioned wall, of rectangular
plan, measuring about a mile and a half each way.
Considerable suburbs prolong to the north, east, and
west the streets which abut on the gates of the
town.   The latter has never been captured by the
Mohammedans, and its inhabitants cherish a fierce
hatred against the rebels of Taly.

The plain of Tchao-tong seems to be the most
extensive in Yunnan, and is carefully cultivated—a

large portion of its area being appropriated to the growth of poppies for the manufacture of opium. Its inhabitants complain of want of water; and, in fact, their only sources of supply are some tiny rills, almost dry in the hot season. There are extensive deposits of anthracite and peat. A small pond, abounding in fish, lies to the south-west.

Tchao-tong is one of the most important commercial *entrepôts* between China and Yunnan. Enormous convoys of raw cotton, of English or native cotton stuffs, and of salt from Se-chuen, are here exchanged for the metals—tin and zinc more particularly—furnished by the environs of Tong-chuen, the medicinal substances which come from the west of Yunnan and the north of Tibet, and the nests of the *coccus sinensis*, which yield the pe-la wax. This insect breeds on a species of privet which grows in the mountainous parts of Yunnan and Se-chuen, and is thence transported to other trees favourable for the production of wax, which flourish in the warmer lowlands. Necessarily, these nests must be conveyed from point to point with great rapidity, lest the newly-hatched insects should die before arriving at their new abode; they are stored away in large baskets, divided into numerous compart-

ments, and their bearers frequently accomplish thirty
or forty leagues at double quick marching step.

Resuming their journey, M. Garnier and his companions traversed a country of great beauty, studded
with villages, and broken up into romantic high-
lands and wooded valleys, watered by copious rivers.
On the 20th of April they reached Lao-oua-tan, a
busy town on the Huang-kiang, at the point where
the navigation of the river begins. Here they
embarked on board a large boat with a capacity of
thirty to forty tons, and began the descent of the
river, admiring the skill with which the Chinese
carried them through the successive rapids. In a
couple of hours they arrived at Pou-eul-tou, a small
port on the left bank, where Garnier and his companions landed, while their baggage and a part of
the escort continued the journey by water. Garnier
pressed forward through a truly Arcadian valley
to Long-ki, the residence of the Vicar-Apostolic
of Yunnan, Monseigneur Ponsot. It is needless
to say that he was received with the warmest
hospitality.

The next stage was Siu-tcheou-fou, a lively and
busy town, where several Roman Catholic mis-

MERCHANT TRAIN IN YUNNAN.

sionaries are stationed. Thence, in a couple of
junks, the travellers descended the Blue River to
Tchong-kin-fou, the great commercial centre of the
province of Se-chuen. Resting here a while, they
then continued their voyage to Han-keou, entering
a region which has been carefully explored and
described by officers of the British navy. The
river all along its course presents an animated scene,
—the junks ascending the stream being towed by
boatmen on the banks, who time their steps to a
rude and noisy song. M. Garnier arrived at Han-
keou on the 4th of June, and once more entered
upon the enjoyment of the comfort and security of
civilized life, after a long, difficult, and perilous
expedition, in which he had added largely to our
knowledge of a region of vast commercial resources.
On the 10th he embarked on board a steamer for
Shanghai,—arriving there on the 12th. After a
week's stay he set out for Saigon; where he presented himself on the 29th, and was received with
the honours due to his courage, his patience, and his
perseverance. He has shown that the Mekong must
hereafter become an important highway of commerce,
and one of the great channels of communication with
Yunnan and Tibet.

CHAPTER IV.

E owe some additional information respecting the great river of Cambodia to Dr. Morice, who travelled in Cochin-China in 1872.

Of the Annamites, the inhabitants of Cochin-China, he says at the outset, that his first feeling with respect to them was one of disgust. Those faces more or less flattened, and often devoid of all intelligence or animation; those livid eyes; and, especially, that broad nose, and those thick upturned lips, reddened and discoloured by the constant use of betel-nut, do not answer to the European ideal of beauty. But after a long acquaintance with them, he, as is the case with other Western visitors, began to discern a glimpse of meaning in most countenances, and even to make distinctions between the ugly ones. He met with some eyes which were not

ANNAMITE LADY AND HER SERVANT.

oblique, some noses which had an almost Caucasian character, and his repugnance gradually disappeared.

Still, from the most favourable point of view, they are a race of low stature and unprepossessing appearance; feeble, deficient in stamina, and never likely to make a noise in the world. Their French rulers grow into giants when compared with these dwarfs; and their muscular energy is far inferior to that of Europeans, whether owing to natural causes or to want of hygienic knowledge. As for their complexion, while some are deeply tinted, others are quite wan and pale. In two respects only can the Annamites be said to surpass their masters : in their ability to row ten hours consecutively, and in the impunity with which they can encounter the burning rays of a tropical sun.

As for their character, it is that of a people whom slavery, ignorance, and sloth have rendered poor, timid, and apathetic. Yet they are capable of being raised to a higher moral and intellectual standard. They have many serious defects, it is true ; they are deficient, for example, in the artistic sentiment. Even of the latter evidence is found in some surprising mural paintings, which reproduce, with loving fidelity, all that is bright and living in nature,

—birds, insects, flowers. But, as a rule, the Annamites are insensible to the arts. Their shrill monotonous music is terrible to a cultured ear; and it may be doubted whether ours is agreeable to them. Of sculpture they know only the rudiments; their poetry is indifferent; they cannot dance. Their literary research is confined to an acquaintance with a few Chinese characters; and their scientific acquirements are a blank.

Then as to their attire. They never abandon their clothes until they fall into rags and tatters, though they are insufficient to protect them against the variations of their climate, and more particularly against the keen frosty mornings of December and January. Their huts or hovels, nearly all built upon piles, half in the water and half in the earth or mud, are singularly unhealthy. The cultivation of rice, and their occupation as fishermen, have rendered them almost amphibious. Water rises frequently to the floor of an Annamite house, particularly in high tides, but it does not discompose the owner; who, in such an event, crouches contentedly on the domestic hearth, or rocks to and fro in his rude hammock, murmuring some monotonous air, or smoking a cigarette shaped like a blunderbuss.

At Saigon (or Sai-gun), the French settlement and seaport, situated at the mouth of a river of the same name, the traveller finds much to interest him. The Botanic Garden, for instance, will well repay inspection, stocked as it is with rare, beautiful, and curious specimens of tropical vegetation. Close at hand lies the so-called Plain of the Tombs; the scene, a century agone, of numerous battles between the inhabitants of Lower Cochin-China and the Annamites; and, between 1860 and 1864, of several engagements between the Annamites and the French. The uniformity of its vast expanse is broken by a number of mounds or tumuli; some on a modest, others on a splendid scale. Constructed of earth or brick, they are covered with a kind of cement, on which are depicted in vivid colours the figures of fantastic animals and impossible plants, while the name and titles of the deceased are inscribed in conspicuous characters.

Here, one day, Dr. Morice chanced to be the spectator of an Annamite funeral, which is always celebrated with a certain amount of pomp, and attended by a numerous train of mourners. The coffin is planted in the centre of a small portable house, made of paper painted in brilliant colours, and cut into curious shapes. A score of bearers carry this miniature temple, resting upon their shoulders the bamboos which support it. A company of persons with torches scatter along the road their prayers to Buddha, traced on golden and silver papers, and set fire to them. In the rear march the friends and relatives of the departed, some uttering forced lamentations, all smiling "in their sleeves;" for these singular people are never so moved by their sorrow that they cannot laugh at a jest, or at any incident of which they immediately seize, as by intuition, the comic side.

Here too he saw some geckos : indeed, they were numerous enough to be considered the genii of the place. Inhabiting the forests and waste places, as well as the huts of the Annamites and the houses of the French, this large lizard, so common in Cochin-China, is one of the animals which give to the fauna of the country its peculiar character. Does the reader know what a gecko is like ? If not, let him try to conceive of a gigantic terrestrial salamander ; its skin, of a bluish-gray, covered with a quantity of tiny tubercles rising in the middle of an

orange-tinted patch; its great eyes having a large
gold-yellow iris; while, owing to the sucker-like
lamellæ that line the under surface of its feet, it is
able to walk easily on the smoothest surfaces, and
utterly to defy the laws of gravitation. Its cry, to
which it owes the name given to it in every language, is curiously sonorous; and when first heard,
fairly startles the hearer. A shaky grumble or
grunt serves as prelude; then, five, six, or eight
times, lowering its voice regularly half a tone on
each occasion, it jerks out its cadenced notes, which
are sometimes written *gecko*, and sometimes *tacke;*
the performance terminating with a grunt of satisfaction.

The gecko grows as familiar with man as the
domestic cat or dog,—entering human habitations
freely, and rendering valuable service by the eager-
ness with which it devours flies, spiders, and other
insect-plagues. During the day, it lurks generally
in some obscure nook or dark corner; but at dusk
sallies forth in search of prey, running up or down
the steepest walls with wonderful swiftness, and
giving utterance to a quick shrill noise by smacking
its tongue against its palate. So flexible is its body,
that it can adapt itself readily to any depression or

irregularity in the surface of the ground, forming apparently a component part of it. This deception is facilitated by its dulness of colouring. It is a home-keeping animal, and never strays to any great distance from the lair which it has chosen. Despite its ugliness and its cry, which at night, when a dozen are heard replying to one another, becomes insupportably wearisome, it is one of man's most useful allies in the animal-world, and merits his respect.

A word as to the formation of its wide feet. All the toes are broadened considerably at the edges, and their under surface is divided into numerous transverse laminæ, from which exudes an adhesive fluid. Its claws are sharp, crooked, and retractile like those of a cat.

Another animal of the same group, but much smaller, and closely resembling the tarenta of which the Toulonese are so afraid, is the *margouilla*, the "con-tan-lan" of the Annamites. It inhabits trees and houses with equal complacency. Every evening, when the tapers are lighted, it may be seen promenading along the ceiling, where it pounces upon the insects, uttering from time to time its short cry of satisfaction, which may be translated by the syllable *toc* ten times repeated. It is partial to sugar; but as it is the inveterate enemy of the mosquitoes, no one begrudges it a dainty morsel from the sugar-basin.

From Saigon Dr. Morice made an excursion to Kholen, the second town in size and population in Cochin-China. It lies about three miles from Saigon, but is connected with it by a line of villages, of pagodas, and of the country-houses of the wealthier Chinese merchants. Kholen is the centre of all the Chinese commerce of the colony. The amount of rice, stuffs, and products exported from China, which is sold there, almost passes belief; and the stranger surveys with interest the animation of its busy streets, and the numerous Chinese junks and Annamite sampans moored alongside its quays.

Among its peculiarities may be specialized its parks or preserves of crocodiles. A barrier of long and solid piles surrounds a space of about twenty square yards on the river-bank; in the mud and slime thus enclosed, and regularly inundated at high water, sprawl from one hundred to two hundred crocodiles. When the people wish to sacrifice one of these monsters, two of the piles are lifted up; a running knot is flung round the neck of the largest of the herd, which is then hauled outside; its tail is fastened close to its body lengthwise; its feet are cut off, and used to garnish its back; the jaws are tied together with ratan; and these vegetable bonds are so firm that the huge creature is incapable of movement, and can offer no defence. As for the flesh, though rather leathery, it appears to have a certain value, and is not so strongly impregnated with the odour of musk as some writers pretend. On Annamite tables it figures as a favourite dish.

From Saigon Dr. Morice's next excursion was to Gocong, which lies in the centre of a district famous for its rice-fields. Thence he made his way to Hatian (or Cancao), of which he gives a lively description furnished to him by a French colonist:—

"Hatian-of-the-Roses is a small gem of flowers and verdure; magnificent pagodas, wooded hills, the limestone mass of Bonnet-à-Poil; everything which one finds nowhere else."

But, says Dr. Morice, he forgot the fever.

There can be no doubt that Hatian is a lovely spot. It is situated on the borders of a lake which opens into the Gulf of Siam; a lake bordered on

CHINESE HOUSE AT KHOLEN

the west by ranges of green hills, luxuriantly clothed with magnificent trees. To the east extends a vast plain, in the centre of which rises the isolated mass of limestone known as the Bonnet-à-Poil. The fields are enamelled with flowers and studded with flowering bushes; and winding paths lead through a succession of scenes of the most various beauty.

The plant chiefly cultivated is the pepper-plant. On a soil raised several feet above the ordinary level are disposed parallel rows of sticks like those which are used in the Kentish hop-gardens, and round each of these coils a vigorous plant. It takes five years for a plant to become productive. Maize is also cultivated, but not to so large an extent.

While Dr. Morice was at Hatian, its Annamite inhabitants celebrated their feast of the *Tét* or New-Year's Day, in which are oddly mingled the religious rites of Buddhism, and the worship of the manes of their forefathers, the fear of the devil or *Maqui*, and the noisiest possible manifestations of popular mirth. It lasts at the least seven days,—with the rich much longer; and the entire settlement gives itself up for this period to the most unrestrained enjoyment.

Before each house, on a table covered with a mat,

is to be seen the offering of meat and drink, rice-spirit in a small white porcelain teapot, tea, betel with all its ingredients, fish, various kinds of Annamite vermicelli, roast duck, a quarter of pork, rice, bananas, and oranges. All this display is set out with flowers; then a couple of small tapers are lighted, and the manes, or domestic spirits, are respectfully invited to come and take their share of the consecrated love-feast. More : on a plate supported on a moderately high post, other and more delicate offerings are displayed,—composed generally of a bouquet of only two species of flowers, the one violet-tinted, the other yellow. As they are seen everywhere, it is probable that a symbolical meaning attaches to the union of these two flowers. Moreover, the rich plant an areca, the poor a large bamboo, in front of the various oblations, and to the top of each fasten a tiny basket of ratan, divided into five compartments. Finally, the altar of Buddha, which forms an indispensable appendage of every hut, is decked out with special pomp; and strips of yellow, red, and violet papers, inscribed with Chinese characters, are affixed to every door. These are intended to avert the presence of the evil spirit during the new year.

Meantime everybody, clothed in their best attire,
—men, women, and children,—that is to say, in a
striped tunic and pantaloons blue, red, yellow, violet,
green, often with the two legs of different colours,
—sallied forth to exchange greetings, or amuse
themselves as best they might. Among the pas-
times most in favour were the following. Javelin-
throwing; in which a long lance of black wood was
made to pass through a ring suspended from a post
about three feet high, and this at a distance of six
to nine yards. This game, which resembles the old
Scotch exercise of tilting at a mark, requires considerable skill on the part of those who engage in
it. Still more popular, especially among women
and children, was the swing, single or double.
And it was not without astonishment that the
traveller found here, in the far East, a kind of
"merry-go-round," such as we see at our fairs and
holiday fêtes, with a score of persons enjoying its
revolutions. There was also the game of shuttle-
cock, which was launched either with hand or foot.
In the midst of all this turmoil might be heard the
monotonous tomtom, the isolated sounds of some
three-stringed guitars, and especially the sharp
reports of petards, which are indispensable at every

festival, and resemble sometimes the file-firing of
infantry.

For this great yearly revel every Annamite saves
up his money for months, and when it comes he
disburses his little store most conscientiously. Frequently an itinerant troop of actors comes—at least
in the principal towns—to contribute its part to the
general rejoicings. As it is the wealthy citizens
who in turn defray the expense of its representa-
tions, we need hardly say that they are very largely
attended. The plays included in their repertory
are always of a noisy character, and plentifully
sprinkled with coarse jokes, at the expense of the
military mandarins, husbands, and especially the
Chinese. Actors hideously painted, with the view
of giving them a formidable appearance, perform in
desperate combats, diversified by guttural cries and
heroic poses of the most ridiculous character.

During his sojourn at Hatian, Dr. Morice paid a
visit to a singularly constructed edifice—the ancient
Chinese palace of the Maqueuou. This Chinese
worthy, it is said, was a simple fisherman; but as
the products of his avocation did not enrich him
with sufficient rapidity, he began to cultivate a little

ground, and started a pepper plantation. One day, while digging, he turned up a store of money,—a supply so ample that it enabled him to bring over to Hatian a large number of his compatriots. He trained them, enrolled them, practised them; and the result was that, one fine morning, Hatian, enriched and largely increased in population, declared itself independent of the empire of Annam, or rather Cambodia, and raised Maqueuou to the throne. He built for himself a splendid palace, and lived for many years afterwards, enjoying the rare pleasure of witnessing the realisation of his dreams. But when he died his organizing genius died with him. Hatian was again annexed to the empire, and the palace fell into ruin; only its four walls are now extant.

The European stranger visits the spot with a feeling of respect for the memory of a bold and energetic man. With some difficulty he clears a path through the luxuriant vegetation, and arrives in front of walls of Cyclopean solidity. Two vast halls, almost choked with balsam, daturas, castor-oil plants, parasites, and refuse, form the entrance. Then come four smaller apartments, in better condition, and each provided with a great circular window.

Here some geckos have established their abode,
saluting the stranger with astonished glances and
piercing cries.

Next comes an immense chamber, almost exactly
square; and several tombs or memorial buildings
are here overshadowed by venerable trees. The
highest, raised in honour of Maqueuou himself,
consists of successive courses of masonry, diminish-
ing gradually from base to summit. Unfortunately,
built of bad materials, it has been seriously injured
by the action of the sun and the rains. A swarm
of bees was domiciled in one of the crannies; and a
tree, the seed of which had probably dropped from
the bill of some wandering bird, soared upward
from the very apex of the pyramid. Four smaller
monuments, all oblong in shape, and traditionally
appropriated to Maqueuou's family, are scattered
around the former. They still bear traces of the
carving with which they were formerly decorated.

Solitude and silence prevail within the precincts
of this vast ruin. The geckos, the birds, and a
squirrel or two, are its only inmates.

Another remarkable object is the so-called pagoda
of Maqui, or the devil. Dr. Morice was greatly
surprised to see appended to its walls a complete

series of water-colour sketches, on very stout paper,
representing the tortures of an Inferno which would
bear comparison with Dante's. The satellites of
the Annamite devil are shown in those pictures as
engaged in the variety of occupations which the old
medieval legends attributed to the imps of Beelzebub.
They are roasting, impaling, cutting to pieces, and
flaying the guilty; throwing them into caldrons of
boiling water, grilling them over fires, and flinging
them to the hungry jaws of enormous tigers.

That Hatian is not without its unpleasant-
nesses, Dr. Morice discovered in an unexpected
fashion. Some workmen, in pulling down an old
wall, came on the lair of a large serpent, which lay
in "multitudinous coils" hatching its store of eggs.
As everybody knew Dr. Morice's zoological tastes,
the workmen sent him immediate information of
their "find," and he quickly arrived- on the spot,
armed with a stick and a long and strong pair of
nippers. Had it not been for its eggs, the animal
would probably have retreated; but it remained
rolled up in its hole, showing only its spotted and
dusky-coloured head. To seize its neck with his
nippers, was Dr. Morice's instant manœuvre; and
then, to the great terror of the Chinese workmen,

he raised it up bodily, and proceeded to carry it off
in triumph. Meanwhile, the irritated creature dis-
charged at its captor's forehead a jet of liquid, from
which, at the time, he felt no disagreeable sensation.
On reaching home, Dr. Morice deposited the reptile
and its eggs in a chest lined with straw; which he
nailed down carefully, and raised above the ground
on vessels of water, as a protection against the attacks
of ants. Then, and not till then, he washed his forehead, bathing, with due caution, the part touched by
the fluid discharge; but still not believing that the
serpent was one of the venomous kind. He troubled
himself no more about his prisoner until, a few days
later, he found in his chamber four tiny serpents,
which he took up in his hand, in spite of their
angry hissing. These he transferred to a glass jar.
The next morning, wishing to examine them, he
was unpleasantly surprised to find them rearing
their head erect and expanding their neck laterally;
and still more disagreeably surprised to detect on
the neck thus expanded the characteristic V. They
belonged to the genus of the spectacled serpent, the
naja of India, the dreaded *cobra capella!*

Dr. Morice hastened to bore some large holes in
the chest containing the serpent and the eggs, and

by means of these he introduced into the interior a
quantity of burning sulphur. When, after a sufficient time had* elapsed, he opened it, he found the
mother and eighteen young ones suffocated, while
four eggs still remained intact. How had the others
been hatched? The circumstance was a novel one,
for it was supposed that only the great serpents—
the pythons and boas—hatched their eggs. At all
events, it was an interesting fact that this animal
had remained faithful to its brood. Among the
sixteen young serpents, only one was a female, and
most of them had already once changed their skin.
They were about thirteen inches long, and their
fangs were clearly discernible. Dr. Morice felt that
he had good reason to be thankful that he had not
been wounded by the *cobra capella* when he so
rashly pounced upon it.

We next find our unwearied travellers under-
taking a journey to Chaudoc, which is situated near
the mouth of the Mekong. On both banks of the
river, but more particularly on the right bank, are
arranged the numerous Annamite huts; and above
them frown the grim walls of a fort, which is in
itself of the size of a small town. The province, of

which Chaudoc is the capital, includes one hundred and five villages, and has a population of eighty-nine thousand souls, of whom eight thousand are Cambodians and sixteen thousand Malays.

Five days later Dr. Morice was at Vinh-Long, the fort of which is equal in magnitude to that of Chaudoc. In the rear of the great muddy moats and embankments of earth, sustained by huge piles, rise the officers' barracks, and the entrenched redoubt containing the soldiers' quarters and the hospital. Bamboos and tall grasses have overgrown a portion of the immense enclosure, and in their tangled mass enormous pythons are frequently killed, while the *najas* lie asleep in the dank inextricable vegetation of the trenches. The town itself is not without a certain agreeableness of aspect; its broad, straight streets are shaded by gigantic cocoa-nut palms.

Still continuing his explorations in the districts watered by the mouths of the Mekong, which forms a considerable delta, traversed by innumerable canals and branches, Dr. Morice arrived at Tayninh, which lies to the east of Saigon. It lines the river-bank for some distance; the houses of the Annamite population being built, not of mud and clay, as in the

VINH-LONG.

western districts of Cochin-China, but of good solid
timber, and with much care and good taste. Their
roofs are also of better construction : instead of the
leaves of the water-palm, a close fine thatch is used,
to which the action of the atmosphere soon gives a
pleasant tint of age. Flourishing coffee-plantations
surround the town, in the rear of which spread the
shadows of a mighty forest, that spreads far up the
sides of a chain of granite mountains of moderate
elevation. The highest of these is the " Black
Lady " (*Nui-ba-dinh*). On the summit, in a picturesque nook, stands a celebrated pagoda, the cells
of its bonzes being excavated out of the neighbouring rock. The pagoda owes its repute to the
neighbourhood of a miraculous spring ; and this
spring rejoices in a legend, which may be told as
follows :—

A bonze of indescribable holiness, who loved to
offer up his prayers in the high places of earth,
climbed the mountain one day in order to make his
devotions on its lofty summit. Despite his sanc-
tity, however, he was human ; and as the mountain was of great elevation and equal barrenness,
he soon grew faint with hunger, but more particularly with thirst. Disdainful, like all sages, of

purely physical needs, he had not taken the precaution of providing himself with these precious necessaries of food and drink, which are the first thought of ordinary mortals. What was he to do? He began to pray; and lo! as he prayed, an enormous rock, which reared its dark front before him, was suddenly cleft open, and revealed to his delighted gaze a crystal spring falling into a basin of stone. From that time the well has never ceased to pour out abundant waters, which heal all the diseases of humanity;—though, strange to say, men, women, and children still die in Cochin-China!

Ten minutes' climbing brought Dr. Morice face to face with this perpetual marvel. His companions hastened to drink copious draughts of the fresh cold water; but Dr. Morice, rejecting the legend, and having less confidence than he ought to have had in temperance principles, resorted to his pocket flask, poured out a glass of French wine, and drank to the majesty of the glorious mountain.

On another occasion Dr. Morice took part in an exciting adventure, which had a painful issue. A tiger, whose depredations had become intolerable, having carried off the best dog of one of the best

SCENE AT TAYNINH.

hunters of the country, it was decided that he must undergo immediate and condign punishment.

The tiger is not often hunted in Cochin-China, where the elephant, that living fortress, does not place at the disposal of the European its high shoulders and formidable tusks. The inhabitants generally resort to snares.

" An expedition having been resolved upon, we surrounded," says Dr. Morice, " the hill which served as a retreat for the monster. More than one hundred and fifty natives were present, shouting, gesticulating, and creating the most awful clamour which ever troubled a tiger's siesta. As for us, the French inspector, a French soldier, and myself, we were in the plain, sprinkled with small mounded graves, which extends behind Tayninh, and waited in patience until it pleased the tiger to show his precious skin. It seemed to be his opinion that the boldest policy was the best; for in less than half an hour after we had drawn our noisy cordon he emerged from the wood, and advanced towards us. He was received with a rolling fire. Of our four balls one at least struck him, for he made a movement of pain, and turned towards the soldier who had accompanied us. That our movements might

be more free, we had separated at some distance
from one another. The soldier immediately leaped
upon a mound about three feet high, and with his
loaded gun in his hand bided the wounded animal's
onset. A second ball from the inspector's rifle hit
him ; but disregarding this new provocation, and
yearning for his prey, he dashed towards the tumu-
lus. With one bound he was at its foot, where he
reared himself erect. Then took place a strange
and lamentable scene, which showed how even the
bravest lose their self-possession when face to face
with these terrible beasts. That the soldier was a
man of courage, numerous incidents had proved: it
was he who had shown the most ardour in organizing the expedition ; he had in his hand a first-rate
rifle, and only the length of his arm apart was the
white chest of the tiger, which seemed to await his
death-dealing bullet. Well, for a few seconds he
contented himself with striking the outstretched
paws before him with the butt-end of his musket.
The tiger extended his body, seized with one of his
claws the unfortunate man's leg, and began to drag
him off."

"A man touched by a tiger is a dead man," says
a German naturalist ; "and it is useless to risk the

life of another in an attempt to snatch from the
cruel beast the mutilated victim whose sufferings
will soon be terminated by death." Such cold-
blooded reasoning never prevails on the scene of
action. Both the doctor and the inspector pursued
the tiger as he still hauled along their comrade's
body; and two bullets, more fortunate than their
predecessors, arrested his course for ever.

On examination, they found that their unfortunate companion had sustained a severe wound. Dr.
Morice amputated his thigh in the hut to which he
was transported; but, whether from loss of blood,
which Europeans can ill afford in tropical latitudes,
or from the violence of the shock to the nervous
system, he died that same night.

From this painful scene it is pleasant to turn to
the market-place of Tayninh, with its various specimens of the human race. Cambodians are toler-
ably numerous; their comparatively tall stature,
their dark skin, their thick and heavy lower jaw,
their hair cut close like the bristles of a brush, and
especially their air of passive savagery, give them
an appearance totally different from that of the
Annamites. The two races detest each other cor-

dially. The Annamite, proud of his lighter complexion, of his more advanced civilization, to say
nothing of the numerous defeats he has inflicted on
his neighbour, looks upon him as little above the
Moïs or wild people of the mountains. The Cambodians are savages, he says, whose nature is radi-
cally bad and vicious; they think nothing of law
or order; they are stupid, and almost devoid of
reason. On the other hand, the Cambodian, with
his gloomier and more silent disposition, his deeper
religious sentiment, regards with compassion the
volatile Annamite. A cordial understanding between the two peoples will hardly ever be possible.
The Cambodian, in spite of his somewhat coarse
features, is more Hindu than Indo-Chinese; and
both his language and his writing have affinities
with those of the aboriginal inhabitants of the great
Indian peninsula. He is the morose and untam-
able denizen of the hills and woods; while his
neighbour is the sociable and light-humoured inha-
bitant of the plains. Unhappy is the Cambodian!
Hemmed in between the Siamese on the one hand,
and the Annamites on the other, who together have
robbed him of his richest provinces; rendered sta-
tionary by the operation of a feudal law which

CHINESE MERCHANTS OF SAIGON.

prevents him from acquiring lands of his own,—a vigorous hand is needed to support him, and enable him to preserve his autonomy, while the ameliorating influences of European civilization are gradually brought to bear upon him.

Such are the two races which occupy the provinces watered by the lower branches of the great Cambodian river. In the large towns and seaports is found a considerable admixture of the Chinese element. Trade and commerce are almost entirely in the hands of Chinese merchants, who, here as elsewhere, exhibit an extraordinary amount of patience, industry, and thrift; and, here as elsewhere, untiringly amass large and even enormous fortunes. They preserve their nationality unaffected by the conditions in which they are placed; always a people apart, and always as distinct from the races around them as are the Jews from the nations of Europe.

CHAPTER V.

UCH of the interesting and valuable information we have acquired of late years in reference to Siam, Cambodia, and Laos, we owe to the indefatigable labours of Henri Mouhot, the eminent French naturalist, who penetrated into regions previously unknown to Europeans in the years 1858, 1859, and 1860, and devoted himself to the service of Science with equal ability and zeal. He finally fell a victim to his heroic ardour—being seized with fever while on his way from Na-Lê to Luang Prabang, in Laos, on the 19th of October 1861, and dying, almost alone, with the exception of two faithful native servants, on the 10th of November.

He spent nearly four years in exploring the interior of Siam. As his biographer tells us, he first travelled through that country, then entered Cambodia, and afterwards made his way up the

Mekong as far as the frontier of Laos. There he visited one of the wild and unconquered tribes which occupy the border-land between Cambodia and Laos and Cochin-China. Crossing the great lake Touli-Sap, he extended his researches into the remote provinces of Ongcor and Battambang, discovering some immense ruins of high antiquity, and more particularly those of the Temple of Ongcor the Great, which, with its terrace, portico, galleries, and peristyles, is perhaps a monument unparalleled in the world. The bas-reliefs with which it is adorned indicate considerable artistic skill on the part of those who designed and executed them. But what impresses the observer, not less than the beauty and grandeur of the various parts of the huge pile, is the size and number of the blocks of stone of which they are constructed. In a single temple as many as fifteen hundred and thirty-two columns! What means of transport, as Mouhot remarks, what a multitude of workmen, must such an enterprise have required, seeing that the mountain whence the stone was extracted is thirty miles distant! In each block may be seen holes an inch in diameter, and an inch and a fifth in depth, varying in number with the size of the blocks; but no traces of them are found in the columns and sculptured portions of the glorious structure. According to a Cambodian legend, these are the impressions of the fingers of a giant, who, after kneading an enormous quantity of clay, cut it into blocks and carved it, and then converted it into stone by pouring over it some wonderful liquid.

"All the mouldings, sculptures, and bas-reliefs," says Mouhot, "appear to have been executed after the erection of the building. The stones are everywhere fitted together in so perfect a manner that you can scarcely see where are the joinings; there is neither sign of mortar nor mark of chisel, the surface being as polished as marble. Was this incomparable edifice the work of a single genius, who conceived the idea, and watched over the execution of it? One is tempted to think so, for no part of it is deficient, faulty, or inconsistent. To what epoch does it owe its origin? As before remarked, neither tradition nor written inscriptions furnish any certain information upon this point; or rather, I should say, these latter are as a sealed book, for want of an interpreter,—and they may, perchance, throw light on the subject when some European savant shall succeed in deciphering them."

From the Mekong valley M. Mouhot passed into that of the great Siamese river, the Menam, visiting the province of Pechaburi. Thence he returned to Bangkok, and after suitable preparation started on an expedition to the north-east of Laos. His wanderings took him to Phrabat, Saohaïe, Chaiapume, and Korat. Returning to Chaiapume, he struck off in a westerly direction, and visited Poukieau, Monang-Mouna-Wa, Nam-kane, and Luang Prabang, capital of West Laos. At the time of his death he was bound for the provinces south-west of China.

It will form, we think, a useful supplement to the account of the Mekong given in the preceding pages, if we condense M. Mouhot's narrative of his partial ascent of that great river.

We will take up our traveller's route at Kamput, on the sea-coast, where he had an interview with the king of Cambodia, and obtained carriages to convey him to Udong, the capital. Udong is situated about one hundred and thirty-five miles to the north-east of Kamput, and four miles and a half from an arm of the Mekong which forms the Great Lake. After traversing a marshy plain he and his followers entered a noble forest, and "under green leaves" proceeded to Udong, resting at night in stations provided for the accommodation of travellers. These are about twelve miles apart, and are not only spacious but handsome. The road all the way proved to be in excellent order, and averaged from eighty to one hundred feet in width. A broad track in the middle is reserved for vehicles and elephants, while on either side extends a belt of turf, covered with shrubs, and bounded by the lofty and majestic trees of the forest. On drawing near the capital, M. Mouhot saw that the country exhibited signs of cultivation: fields of rice waved luxuriantly, and the country residences of the Cambodian nobles were surrounded by beautiful gardens. The capital was protected by a large moat, surmounted by a parapet, and enclosed by a palisade ten feet high. There were no sentinels at the gate, however, and M. Mouhot entered unchallenged; nay, more, without let or hindrance passed into the palace-court of the second king of Cambodia.

This distinguished personage soon heard of the stranger's arrival, and despatched a couple of pages to summon him to his presence. Mouhot would have excused himself on the plea that his luggage had not arrived, and he was not in suitable attire.

He was told that the king had no dress at all; and before he could invent a second excuse, the king's chamberlain arrived with a more peremptory message. Mouhot, therefore, repaired to the palace, the entrance of which was guarded by a dozen dismounted cannon, and was shown into the audience-chamber, the walls of which were whitened with chalk, and the floor paved with large Chinese tiles. Here, waiting for the king's appearance, were collected several Siamese pages, from twenty-five to thirty years of age, all dressed alike in a langouti of red silk. As the king entered every forehead touched the ground. His manner was graceful and self-possessed, and the questions he asked were pertinent and sensible. Was M. Mouhot French or English? What was his business in Cambodia? What did he think of Bangkok? Then, with all the ease of a European sovereign, he held out his hand for Mouhot to kiss; and the latter withdrew, well pleased with the interview.

An inspection of the city showed him that it contained a population of about twelve thousand souls; that it consisted in the main of a street one mile in length; and that the houses were built of planks or bamboos. It presents a very lively appearance,

however, from the numbers of persons who are
drawn to it by considerations of business or pleasure. "Every moment," says Mouhot, "I met
mandarins, either borne in litters or on foot, followed
by a crowd of slaves carrying various articles : some,
yellow or scarlet parasols, more or less huge according to the rank of the persons ; others, boxes with
betel. I also encountered horsemen, mounted on
pretty, spirited little animals, richly caparisoned
and covered with bells, ambling along, while a troop
of attendants, covered with dust and sweltering with
heat, ran after them. Light carts, drawn by a
couple of small oxen, trotting along rapidly and
noisily, were here and there to be seen. Occasionally a large elephant passed majestically by. On
this side were numerous processions to the pagoda,
marching to the sound of music ; there, again, was
a band of ecclesiastics in single file, seeking alms,
draped in their yellow cloaks, and with the holy
vessels on their backs."

From Udong, with waggons and elephants provided by the king, M. Mouhot proceeded towards
the Great Lake. The road was in excellent condition, and at some points built up more than ten

feet above the level of the low, wooded country
which borders on the great arm of the Mekong.
The watercourses were spanned by handsome bridges
of wood or stone. At Pinhalu, a village on the
right bank of the river, is the residence of the
French Vicar-Apostolic of the Cambodia and Laos
mission. Here our traveller embarked in a small
boat for Pemptielan, situated on the Mekong, about
forty miles north of Pnom Penh. The branch which
he descended was fifteen hundred yards wide, and its
banks were inhabited by a tribe called the Thiâmes.
Pnom Penh, which Mouhot reached after a perilous
voyage, is the great bazaar of Cambodia. It contains a population of about ten thousand, nearly
all Chinese ; while double that number of Cochin-
Chinese and Cambodians live upon the river in their
boats. An active trade is carried on here in rice,
fish, glass, brass wire, and cotton yarn.

Just below this busy town M. Mouhot's boat
passed into the main channel of the Mekong—the
"Mother of Rivers"—and began to ascend it,
steering towards the north. Shoals of porpoises
accompanied it, occasionally bounding out of the
water with a lively splash ; red - billed pelicans
watched for their finny prey from the reedy

banks; and storks and herons stood in silent medi-
tation.

The current of the Mekong, as we have already
stated, flows with great rapidity, and renders navigation slow and laborious. It took M. Mouhot five
days to pass the island of Ko-Sutin; and the rate of
velocity increasing as he advanced to the northward,
he was seldom able to accomplish more than two
miles a day. On arriving at the rapids and cata-
racts he was compelled to abandon his boats and
embark, with his followers and stores, in light canoes;
and even these it was necessary at times to carry
ashore, and convey along the bank on men's shoulders until a smooth part of the river was gained.

At Pemptielan Mouhot landed, and delivered to
its mandarin a letter from the king, ordering him to
furnish the traveller with all the appliances requisite
for his overland journey. He immediately started
him on his way with a suitable number of waggons
drawn by oxen, but the soil in the forests was so
marshy that they were continually sinking in some
deep slough, from which they could be extricated
only by the greatest exertions. Thus their progress
was limited to sixty miles in five days. At length
he reached the village of Brelum, in the centre of

a district occupied by the savage Stiêns. Here, in order to study their manners and the physical features of the country, he remained three months, though it is difficult to conceive of a situation less pleasing to or suitable for a man of European culture. The gloomy forests around were infested with elephants, rhinoceroses, tigers, buffaloes, and wild boars. More formidable, because less easily avoided, were the snakes, scorpions, and centipedes which swarmed in every direction, and constantly made their way into the houses. Brelum, however, is the seat of a Roman Catholic mission, and from its head, Father Guilloux, the traveller received a cordial hospitality which alleviated the dreariness of his sojourn.

He describes the Stiêns as dwelling in villages, each of which forms a distinct and independent community. They love "the deep shade of the pathless woods," where they live on the products of their bow and arrows. They work with great skill in iron and ivory; and the women weave and dye a delicate stuff, which they wear in the form of a long loose scarf. In the neighbourhood of their villages, if the country be open, they cultivate various kinds of vegetables and fruit-trees, as well as rice, maize, and tobacco. In the fields thus planted they spend the rainy season, building small huts, raised above the swampy ground on piles—a protection at once from the swollen waters and the leeches, the latter of which are a plague of no inconsiderable proportions.

There is a certain peculiarity in their method of cultivating rice. On the beginning of the rains the Stiên selects his piece of ground, and with nimble hatchet clears it of its growth of bamboos, but not attempting to meddle with the large trees. As soon as the canes have dried he sets fire to them, and in this way clears his ground and manures it simultaneously. Then he takes two long bamboos and lays them in a line on the ground ; with a dibble in each hand he makes on either side a row of holes about an inch and a half deep, at short distances. Having finished *his* share of the work the man retires to enjoy his ease, while his wife enters on the scene, and from a basket slung to her waist dips out a handful of rice, a few grains of which she drops into each hole with equal neatness and rapidity. No more is necessary. Nature does the rest. The heavy rains soon wash the soil over the holes; and the heat of the climate soon causes the seed to germinate. Meanwhile the cultivator sits and smokes in his hut, or proves his skill with bow and arrow at the expense of the goats, apes, or wild boars. At the end of October is reaped the harvest. Generally, for some weeks previously much privation and distress are experienced, and the improvident Stiên, who never takes thought of the morrow in the season of plenty, is reduced to feed upon wild roots, maize seeds, young bamboo shoots, and even serpents, bats, and toads. For this sorry fare the Stiên compensates himself as soon as the harvest is gathered. A general feasting commences: one village inviting the inhabitants of another; oxen being freely slaughtered; and eating and drinking prevailing from morn to night, and almost from night to morn, to the sound of tambourine and tomtom.

Like the Annamites, the Stiêns wear the hair long, but twisted up, and fastened by a bamboo comb, with a pheasant's crest on the top of a piece of brass wire by way of ornament. They are mostly of tall stature, strong, and well-limbed; with regular features, thick eyebrows, and a good forehead. Their hospitality is abundant, and a stranger, on his arrival, is immediately entertained with rice-wine, a pipe of

peace, and a fatted pig or fowl. Their dress is sim-
plicity itself,—a long scarf about two inches wide;
and even with this they dispense when "at home"
in their cabins. They have neither priests nor
temples ; and their religion appears to consist of a
belief in a supreme being called *Brâ;* to whom, on
occasions of calamity and suffering, they sacrifice a
pig or an ox, and sometimes a human victim.

They are very careful in burying their dead; and
a member of the family of the deceased invariably
visits the grave daily, to sow a few grains of rice for
his sustenance. Prior to any meal, they spill a little
rice for the same purpose; and similar offerings are
made in the fields and places which the dead were
accustomed to visit. Plumes of reed are attached to
the top of a long bamboo, and lower down the stem
are fastened smaller bamboos containing a few drops
of wine or water; and, finally, on "a slight trellis-
work raised above the ground" some earth is laid, with
an arrow planted in it, and a few grains of cooked
rice, a leaf, a little tobacco, and a bone spread about.

The Stiêns believe that animals have souls; that
these wander about after death; and that, therefore,
it is necessary to propitiate them, lest they should be
troublesome and vexatious. Sacrifices are accord-

ingly offered, in proportion to the size and strength
of the animal ; and the reader will conceive that
in the case of an elephant they are on a very grand
scale. The North American Indian, it may be remarked, cherishes a similar superstition in respect to
the bear and the buffalo.

According to M. Mouhot, a Stiên is seldom seen
without his cross-bow in his hand, his knife slung
over his shoulder, and a basket—for his arrows, and
the game they bring down—on his back. In the
chase he displays the most untiring energy, gliding
through the woods "with the speed of a deer." In
the use of the cross-bow practice brings perfection.
For the larger animals the arrows are steeped in a
poison which is described as being peculiarly rapid
and fatal in its effects.

The Stiêns, let it be said in conclusion, are, like
most savage races, exceedingly partial to ornaments,
. and particularly to bracelets made of bright-coloured
beads. The men usually wear one above the elbow,
and one at the wrist ; but the women load both
arms and legs. Brass wire and glass ornaments
form their currency; a buffalo or an ox being valued
at six armfuls of thick brass wire, which is also
about the price of a pig. A pheasant, however, or

a hundred ears of maize, may be procured for a small piece of fine wire or a bead necklace.

Both men and women perforate their ears, widening the hole annually by the insertion of plugs of bone or ivory fully three inches in length. A plurality of wives is allowed to the chiefs and richer men of the tribe; the poor are content with one wife, simply because they cannot afford to maintain a harem.

About the fauna of this portion of the Mekong valley little need be said, and that little we shall confine to the tiger, which is as strong and ferocious as his celebrated congener of Bengal. Yet a couple of men, with no other weapons than pikes, will frequently sally forth to the attack. When the object of their daring enterprise is discovered, the stronger of the two hunters lowers his pike. Sometimes, if not emboldened by hunger, the tiger refuses the challenge, and bounds into the forest shade; more frequently he charges with a sudden rush, and then, if the force of his leap do not carry him over the head of the hunter, he falls upon the pike, which the hunter raises by pressing the handle on the earth. Immediately his companion rushes forward, and plunges his weapon into the animal's flank; then the two, by sheer force, pin him to the ground, and hold him there until he dies. If the first man miss his aim, and break his pike, his death is certain; and not seldom his comrade also perishes.

But generally a tiger-hunt brings to the front all the men of the village, together with volunteers from the neighbouring villages. Led by the most experienced among them, they track the animal to his lair, which they proceed to enclose with a circle— each man being posted at a convenient distance, but so as to leave no space unguarded through which the tiger may escape. "Some of the most daring then venture into the centre," says Mouhot, "and cut away the brushwood, during which operation they are protected by others armed with pikes. The tiger, pressed on all sides, rolls his eyes, licks his paws in a convulsive manner as though preparing for combat; then, with a frightful howl, he makes his spring. Immediately every pike is raised, and the animal falls pierced through and through. Accidents not infrequently happen, and many are often severely hurt; but they have no choice but to wage war against the tigers, which leave them no rest, force the enclosures, and carry off domestic animals and even men, not only from the roads and close vicinity of the houses, but from the interiors of the buildings. In Annam, the fear inspired by the tigers, elephants, and other wild animals, makes the people address them with the greatest respect; they give them the title of 'grandfather' or 'lord,' fearing that they may be offended, and show resentment by attacking them." It is a pity that poets and romancists, when enlarging on the joys of a savage life, its freedom from the restraints of civilization, and the opportunities it affords for communion with Nature, omit all reference to its inconveniences,—such, for instance, as the immediate neighbourhood of an elephant or a tiger!

After a sojourn of three months among the Stiêns, M. Mouhot returned to Udong by the route which he had previously followed. Of Pnom Penh, he says that it is situated at the confluence of the Mekong with its tributary, which he proposes to name the Mé-Sap. This arm or tributary it is which forms the great Cambodian lake Touli-Sap; an immense sheet of water, upwards of one hundred and twenty miles in length, and four hundred miles in circumference, and as full of motion as a sea.

Its shores are low, and covered with half-submerged trees; but in the distance may be seen a magnificent range of mountains, with the clouds resting on their summits.

To the east of the Great Lake lies the province of Ongcor, or Nokhor, in which, and along the banks of the Mekong, lie ruins of immense grandeur, bearing witness to the ancient wealth and populousness of the kingdom of Tsiampois (Cochin-China). To the most remarkable of these monuments, the great temple of Ongcor-Wat, we have already alluded. Its founders are unknown. Ask the Cambodians, and they reply: "It is the work of Pra-Enn, the king of the angels;" or else, "It is the work of giants;" or, "It was built by the leper King;" or, "It made itself."

Two miles and a half to the north of Ongcor, on the summit of Mount Bakhêng, rises another magnificent Buddhist temple, not less than one hundred and twenty feet in height. At the foot of the mountain two stately lions, each formed, with its pedestal, out of a single block of limestone, keep watch in the silent shadows of the forest-trees. Thence dilapidated stone staircases lead to the mountain-top, from which a view of singular beauty and extent is obtained. On the one side are visible the wooded plain and pyramidal temple of Ongcor, with its noble colonnades, and the mountain of Crôme,—the horizon being bounded by the shining waters of the Great Lake. In the opposite direction extends the long mountain-chain, the quarries of which, it is said, supplied the materials of the temples; and among the dense masses of foliage at its feet glimmers a fair and silvery lake. The entire region is now as lonely and deserted as formerly it must have been full of life and cheerfulness. The solitude is disturbed only by the occasional song of bird, or wild, unearthly cry of beast of prey.

A smooth surface has been obtained on the top of the mountain by laying down a thick floor of lime. At regular intervals are four rows of deep holes, in some of which still stand the columns that formerly supported two roofs, and formed a corridor leading from the staircase to the body of the building. The arms or branches of this gallery were connected with four towers, built partly of stone and partly of brick. In the two of these which are in the best preservation are kept large rudely-fashioned idols, evidently of great antiquity. In one of the others is a large stone, with an inscription still visible;

the figure of a king with a long beard is carved upon the outer wall.

A wall, says Mouhot, surrounds the top of the mountain, and encloses yet another building—quadrangular in shape, and composed of five stories, each about ten feet high, while the basement story is two hundred and twenty feet square. These stories form so many terraces, which serve as bases to seventy-two small but elegant pavilions; and they are embellished with mouldings, colonnades, and cornices. M. Mouhot describes the work as perfect; and is of opinion that, from its good state of preservation, it must be of later date than the towers. Each pavilion, it may be assumed, formerly contained an idol.

On either side of the quadrangle ascends a staircase, seven feet wide, with nine steps to each story, and lions on each terrace. The centre of the terrace formed by the last story is simply a mass of ruins from the shattered towers. Near the staircase lie two gigantic blocks of fine stone, wrought as smooth as marble, and shaped like pedestals for statues.

[So far from M. Mouhot. It will be interesting, however, to supplement his description with the details given by Lieutenant Garnier.

The ascent of the so-called mountain, he says, is
easily accomplished : after a little time the traveller
arrives at a kind of platform excavated in the rock,
the surface of which appears formerly to have been
carefully levelled with cement. A small brick building attracts the eye ; it is erected over the imprint
of Buddha's foot, the gilding and outlines of which
are, like the building itself, of very modern date.
But we soon discover, in the rock, numerous holes
which served as foundations for the columns of the
temple; and beyond, some of these columns are still
standing. If we follow up the traces of this colonnade, we arrive at an enclosure which was opened
of old, perhaps, by a monumental gate ; but there
are not sufficient vestiges extant to enable us safely
to reconstruct this part of the edifice. Within the
enclosure, and symmetrically placed on either side
of the colonnade, we find two ruined buildings; and
in their interior numerous statues and fragments of
statues have been carefully preserved by the inhabitants. Continuing our exploration westward, we
arrive at length at the foot of the principal monument. This consists of five terraces excavated on
the crest of the hill in exact gradation. Their
general plan is rectangular, and one recedes behind

the other at least thirteen feet. We ascend them by means of staircases constructed in the middle of each side, and guarded by stone lions mounted upon pedestals. At the angle of each terrace, and about thirty feet from each staircase, are raised admirably built little turrets, sixteen feet in height. Each of these sixteen turrets contains a statue.

In the centre of the upper terrace is a platform or base, about three and a quarter feet high, and measuring one hundred feet from north to south by one hundred and three feet from east to west. On this base were raised of old the towers which dominated the neighbouring country. But it is occupied now by a mass of ruins. By carefully examining them, we are able to make out that these towers were three in number, of which the central was the largest, and that they faced the east. The view from the summit of the ruins is truly enchanting. At our feet extends the verdurous sea of forest, its vague and undefinable murmurs just audible to the attentive ear. In a northerly direction the dense forest-shadows stretch far and far away until lost in the dim horizon; and the eye seeks vainly to discover in its midst the crests of some of the lofty monuments of Ongcor. To the south-east, however, the towers and colonnades of Ongcor-Wat are clearly marked out upon the great open plain; and the few groves of palms and clusters of fruit-trees which surround it give to the landscape an Oriental character of poetry and grace. Westward, a small lake reflects in its glassy surface the surrounding verdure. To the south we catch glimpses, through the warm vapours which veil the horizon, of the Great Lake.

What a fairy-like aspect, from the summit of these towers, must the mountain itself, in the old time, have presented, with its lions, and its turrets, and its staircases of stone descending even to the plain and to the city of Ongcor-Thôm, with its ramparts and its innumerable gilded towers, which the forest now covers with its vast monotonous shroud of verdure!

From the extent of the débris accumulated at the foot of the monument, we may conjecture that formerly a double row of buildings of brick surrounded it; these were probably occupied by a garrison or a numerous military guard. The position of Mount Bakhêng with reference to the neighbouring city made it a kind of Acropolis; and doubtless it was so used from the very foundation of the city. But while Mouhot ascribes the monument which it supports to the very infancy of Cambodian art, the leader of Garnier's expedition considered it of later date. The fashion of the ornamentation and the style of the architecture seemed to him almost identical with those of other Khmer ruins. Moreover, in his opinion this architecture sprang into existence, so to speak, all at once ; was complete in itself; had neither a period of development nor one of decay;—as if it had been introduced from without by a conquering race, which afterwards had been swept away by some sudden catastrophe.]

After a careful survey of the ruins of Ongcor and Ongcor-Thôm (or "the Great"), M. Mouhot returned to Bangkok, and made preparations to visit the north-eastern provinces of Laos.

While at Bangkok he witnessed a succession of fêtes, of which he records details so interesting, that, by way of digression, we venture to transfer them to these pages.

The river Menam, he says, was covered with large and handsome boats, gay with gilding and gorgeous with elaborate carving ; among which the

heavy barges of the rice-merchants, and the small
craft of poor women carrying to market their betel-
nuts and bananas, seemed out of place.   It is only
on such occasions as these that the king, princes,
and mandarins display their wealth and pomp.   The
king, when Mouhot saw him, was proceeding to a
pagoda to make his offerings; and was followed by
his mandarins, each in a splendid barge, with rowers
attired in the brightest colours.   In their train came
a number of canoes filled with red-coated soldiers.
The royal barge was easily distinguished by its
throne and canopy, and by the profuseness of its
carving and gilding.   Some of the royal children
sat at the feet of the king, who waved a recognition
to every European he saw.

All the vessels lying in the river were dressed
out with flags; while every floating house had an
altar erected, on which various objects were placed,
and aromatic woods burned with pleasant odours.
In the court barges the various dignitaries, mostly
men of "good round paunch," lay indolently upon
triangular embroidered cushions spread on a kind
of dais.   They were surrounded by officials, women,
and children, either kneeling or lying flat, and
holding the golden urns which are used for spit-

toons, or the golden tea-pots and betel-boxes. Each boat carried from eighty to a hundred rowers, wearing a large white scarf round the loins, and a red langouti, but leaving the head and greater part of the body bare. They lifted their paddles simultaneously, and struck the water in excellent concert; while at the prow stood a slave with an oar to prevent collisions, and another at the stern employed an oar for steering purposes. At intervals the rowers raised "a wild, exulting cry of 'Ouah! ouah!'" while the voice of the steersman, in a louder and more sustained note, rose above the rest.

From this holiday city, however, M. Mouhot tore himself away, and entered on his lonely and hazardous journey. He soon reached the pure breezy air and picturesque scenery of the mountains of Nophaburi and Phrabat, and ascended the Menam to Saohaïe, the starting-point for all caravans going to Korat. He thence continued his voyage to Khao-Khoc, which has been fortified by the king of Siam as an asylum in case of a European invasion of the south. Here he resided for some months, on the borders of a vast unexplored forest, studying the manners and customs of the Laotians. In February 1861 he arrived at Chaiapune. It was not until he had encountered and conquered obstacles that would have broken the heart of any man less enthusiastic or less courageous that he succeeded in making his way to Korat. As he describes it as "a nest of robbers and assassins, the resort of all the scum of the Laotian and Siamese races," the rendezvous of "bandits and vagrants escaped from slavery or from prison," he would hardly have found it a pleasant resting-place; and as soon as he could obtain a supply of elephants for himself and his followers, he resumed his journey, striking across the country to Poukicau.

Here he ascended gradually a range of mountains abounding in resinous trees and frequented by deer, tigers, elephants, and rhinoceros. This chain extends directly north, continually increasing in height and breadth, and throwing off numerous spurs towards the east, where the deep shadowy valleys collect their waters, and pour them into the Mekong.

Throughout this mountainous region elephants are the only means of transport. Every village, consequently, possesses one of these valuable animals; some no fewer than fifty or a hundred.

Otherwise, intercommunication would be impossible for seven months out of the twelve. "The elephant," says Mouhot, "ought to be seen on these roads, which I can only call devil's pathways, and are nothing but ravines, ruts two or three feet deep, full of mud; sometimes sliding with his feet close together on the wet clay of the steep slopes, sometimes half-buried in mire,—an instant afterwards mounted on sharp rocks where one would think a Blondin alone could stand; striding across enormous trunks of fallen trees, crushing down the smaller trees and bamboos which oppose his progress, or lying down flat on his stomach, that the cornacs (drivers) may the easier place the saddle on his back; a hundred times a day making his way, without injuring them, between trees where there is barely room to pass; sounding with his trunk the depth of the water in the streams or marshes; constantly kneeling down and rising again, and never making a false step. It is necessary, I repeat, to see him at work like this in his own country, to form any idea of his intelligence, docility, and strength, or how all these wonderful joints of his are adapted to their work—fully to understand that this colossus is no rough specimen of Nature's handiwork,

but a creature of especial amiability and sagacity,
designed for the service of man."

After leaving Korat, Mouhot crossed five considerable rivers,—the Menam-Chic, the Menam-
Leuye, the Menam-Ouan, the Nam-Pouye, and the
Nam-Houn,—all tributaries of the mighty Mekong;
and the last-named river he once more reached, at
Pak Lay, in lat. 19° 16' 58", on June the 24th,
1861. The Mekong here is much broader than the
Menam at Bangkok, and dashes through the mountain ravine with the impetuosity of a torrent and
the roar of the sea. Its navigation between Pak
Lay and Luang Prabang is interrupted by several
rapids.

Luang Prabang, where Mouhot arrived on the
25th of July, is a pleasantly-situated town, occupy-
ing an area of one square mile, and containing
a population of eight thousand. The mountains
which, both above and below it, enclose the broad
and copious Mekong, form at this point a kind of
circular valley or amphitheatre, nine miles in diameter, and, with their woods, and luxuriant verdure,
and lawny slopes, combine in a picturesque panorama, reminding one of the Alpine lakes.

The town extends on both banks of the stream,

but chiefly on the left bank, where the houses surround an isolated mount about three hundred and
fifty feet in height, covered by a pagoda.*

An important tributary of the Mekong, the Nam
Kan, skirts on the east and north the little hill at
the foot of which Luang Prabang is situated, and
divides the latter into two unequal parts, the larger
of which lies to the south of the point of confluence.
The banks of this stream, for a considerable distance
inland, are lined with an uninterrupted series of
pagodas and great gardens, in the latter of which
the betel-nut is cultivated, and peaches, plum-trees,
and oleanders flourish: a sign that the traveller here
enters a very temperate region, where the fruits and
plants of Central Asia may be successfully cultivated.

In the southern district of the city is placed the
palace of the king, an enormous aggregate of huts,
enclosed by a high and strong palisade, and forming
a rectangle, one side of which is contiguous to the
base of the central mount. As this sacred hillock is
there almost perpendicular, the ascent to its pagoda-
crowned summit is effected by a flight of several
hundred steps excavated in the rock. A daily and

* A fuller description of Luang Prabang, as given by Garnier, who visited it
six years after Mouhot, will be found on page 78.

excessively animated market is held under some
sheds situated near the junction of the Nam Kan
and the Mekong; but they are insufficient to accom-
modate all the vendors, and open booths, stalls, or
shops are prolonged for upwards of half a mile in a
wide street parallel to the river.

M. Garnier remarks that this was the first market,
in the European sense of the word, which he had
seen since leaving Pnom Penh. This sudden activity,
he adds, and comparatively considerable commerce,
to judge from the numerous and diverse types which
at Luang Prabang represented all the nations of
Indo-China and India, were obviously due less to a
change of race or increased product of the soil than
to a radical difference of government. The countries of Southern Laos, in their era of independence,
had been celebrated for their wealth and commercial
enterprise ; but Siamese tyranny and monopoly
have blighted their prosperity. If life be reviving
at Luang Prabang, it is because the Siamese court
have awakened to a perception of the fact that a
milder rule was essential for so powerful a province.

The foundation of Luang Prabang appears to date
only from the early part of the eighteenth century.
No reference to it occurs in the careful account of

Siam compiled by the Jesuit missionary La Loubère
in 1687–88. Its distance from the theatre of the
wars which desolated Indo-China in the eighteenth
century, greatly contributed to assure its prosperity, and was probably one of the principal causes
which led to its foundation. Its government skil-
fully contrived to obtain the nominal protection of
China, by sending an envoy once every eight years
with a couple of elephants, as a sign of homage;
and it has secured the goodwill of the Annamite
empire, by consenting to pay a small triennial tribute.
The mountainous country to be traversed before an
army can reach Luang Prabang, and the energy
which its population owes to the admixture of
numerous savage and warlike tribes inhabiting the
borders of Tonquin and Laos, invest this province
with exceptional means for resisting aggression on
the part of Siam.

But we have exhausted our space; and, after
leading the reader into territories which have before
them a splendid future, and following with him
the course of the great Cambodian river into regions
almost unknown to Europeans—regions the resources
of which are immense, but need the science and

energy of Europe for their development—we must bring our narrative to a close.

We have accompanied Mouhot to Luang Pra-bang. Thence he returned to Pak Lay, where, he says, he had the pleasure of again seeing the beautiful stream which he had come to regard as an old friend. "I have so long drunk of its waters," he writes ; "it has so long either cradled me on its bosom or tried my patience,—at one time flowing majestically among the mountains, at another muddy and yellow as the Arno at Florence."

Revisiting Luang Prabang on the 25th of July, he left it again on the 9th of August. A few months later his adventurous career, as we have already stated, was terminated by an attack of jungle fever.

Hitherto, it has been to the research and adventure of French travellers that geographers have principally owed their knowledge of the Mekong. Let us hope that before long some Englishmen will follow in their steps!

THE END.

THE FAC-SIMILE SERIES OF

"𝔒𝔵𝔣𝔬𝔯𝔡" 𝔗𝔢𝔞𝔠𝔥𝔢𝔯𝔰' 𝔅𝔦𝔟𝔩𝔢𝔰

WITH 50,000 REFERENCES

has received the universal approbation of the MINISTRY, the PRESS, and the PUBLIC, and is conceded by ALL to be the very BEST " TEACHERS' BIBLE " in the market.

From the "SUNDAY SCHOOL TIMES."

In an OXFORD BIBLE one is always sure of a good thing. The OXFORD PRESS has done good service by the issue of these TEACHERS' BIBLES, with their full and admirable series of helps. So far as we can see, the new *fac-simile* series of Oxford Bibles for Sunday school Teachers is, all things considered, better suited to the wants of the Sunday School Teacher than any other series yet offered to the public. In typography, paper, binding, varied and excellent helps to study, these Bibles are with the very foremost; and their range of styles and prices gives a choice to all.

From the "NORTH-WESTERN ADVOCATE."

OXFORD BIBLES are printed from *standing* type, *not* from plates. The OXFORD PRESS cast their own types, make their own paper from rags *only*, and bind their books themselves. The manipulation of a genuine OXFORD BIBLE, both as to paper and binding, will satisfy the most minute scrutiny. The clearness of the printed page leaves nothing to be desired. As to the binding, the book *may be doubled flat back, may be thrown down and even trampled upon, without a leaf starting, or it may be suspended by a single leaf without sustaining injury.* The back of the book is so supple it *cannot be broken*, and in order to take the book to pieces, the leaves must be torn out separately. The paper itself possesses a toughness which cannot be surpassed, but the binding will, for durability, outlast the paper. The information contained in the Notes, etc., is nearly all new, or rewritten in such a way as to embrace the greatest amount of knowledge in the smallest compass. The most eminent scholars and professors of OXFORD UNIVERSITY have been employed on these articles, and they have been revised by the most eminent Divines, so as to make the matter as perfect as possible, and acceptable to *all*.

For Prices, Sizes, etc., see next pages.

PRICES AND SIZES

OF THE FAC-SIMILE SERIES OF

"𝔒𝔵𝔣𝔬𝔯𝔡" 𝔗𝔢𝔞𝔠𝔥𝔢𝔯𝔰' 𝔅𝔦𝔟𝔩𝔢𝔰

WITH 50,000 REFERENCES.

PEARL 24mo. (Size 4 x 5½ x 1¾ inches.) Postage, 9 cents.

NOS.

500	French Morocco, gilt edge, stiff covers, silk book mark........	$1 50
501	French Morocco, " circuit covers, " "	1 75
502	Venetian Morocco, " " " "	2 00
505	Persian Morocco, " flexible covers," "	2 10
508	Imitation Seal Skin, " Divinity circuit, silk sewed, lined with leather, and band..........	2 50
510	Turkey Morocco gilt edge, stiff covers........	2 60
511	Turkey Morocco, " flexible covers.....................	2 60
512	Turkey Morocco, " circuit covers.....................	3 50
515	Levant Morocco, " Divinity circuit, kid-lined and band, *silk sewed*, flexible back..........................	4 60

PEARL 8vo. (Size 4 x 6½ x 1¾ inches.) Postage, 12 cents.

815	Levant Morocco, Divinity circuit, kid-lined and band, *silk sewed*, flexible back..........................	$5 75
816	Levant Morocco, Divinity circuit, kid-lined and band, *best* silk sewed, flexible back..........	7 25

RUBY 16mo. (Size 4 x 6½ x 1½ inches.) Postage, 12 cents.

565	Levant Morocco, Divinity circuit, kid-lined and band, silk sewed, flexible back	$5 25
566	Levant Morocco, Divinity circuit, kid-lined and band, *best* silk sewed, flexible back, red and gold edges	6 75

Other styles are in preparation and will be ready shortly.

NONPAREIL 16mo. (Size 4 x 6¼ x 1¾ inches.) Postage, 12 cents.

600	French Morocco, gilt edges, stiff covers, silk book mark........	$2 35
601	French Morocco, " circuit covers, " "	2 75
605	Persian Morocco, " flexible covers," "	2 75
608	Imitation Seal Skin, " Divinity circuit, silk sewed, lined with leather, and band.........	3 50
610	Turkey Morocco, gilt edges, stiff covers.....................	3 25

611 Turkey Morocco, gilt edges, flexible covers $3 25
612 Turkey Morocco,   "   circuit covers.......... . ... 4 50
615 Levant Morocco,   "   Divinity circuit, kid-lined and
     band, silk sewed, flexible back............... .... 5 75
616 Levant Morocco, Divinity circuit, kid-lined and band, *best* silk
     sewed, flexible back, red and gold edges............ ... .. 7 25

NONPAREIL 8vo. (Size 4½ x 7 x 1¾ inches.) Postage, 16 cents.

661 Turkey Morocco, gilt edges, flexible covers..................$4 25
665 Levant Morocco, Divinity circuit, kid-lined and band, silk
     sewed, flexible back..................... .. .. 6 75
666 Levant Morocco, Divinity circuit, kid-lined and band, *best* silk
     sewed, flexible back, red and gold edges....... .... 8 25
Other styles are in preparation and will be ready shortly.

MINION 8vo. (Size 5 x 7¾ x 1½ inches.) Postage, 18 cents.

705 Persian Morocco, gilt edges, flexible covers..................$4 25
708 Imitation Seal Skin, gilt edges, Divinity circuit, silk sewed,
     lined with leather, and band............................... 5 25
710 Turkey Morocco, gilt edges, stiff covers................. . 5 00
711 Turkey Morocco,   "   flexible covers............. .. .... 5 00
715 Levant Morocco,   "   Divinity circuit, kid-lined and
     band, silk sewed, flexible back 7 50
716 Levant Morocco, Divinity circuit, kid-lined and band, *best* silk
     sewed, flexible back, red and gold edges......... ....10 25
718 Seal Skin, Divinity circuit, kid-lined and band, *best* silk sewed,
     flexible back, red and gold *solid* edges.................... 14 00

LARGE MARGIN, MINION 8vo, FOR MSS. NOTES.
Postage, 28 cents.

905 Persian Morocco, gilt edges, stiff covers.............. ....$7 50
910 Turkey Morocco,   "   stiff covers................. . ...10 50
911 Turkey Morocco,   "   flexible covers..... .. ..10 50
915 Levant Morocco   "   Divinity circuit, kid-lined and
     band, silk sewed, flexible back.. .. ..14 00

For samples of type and further information apply to all Booksellers,
or to

THOMAS NELSON & SONS,

Agents for the Oxford University Bible House,

42 BLEECKER ST., NEW YORK.

Sunday School Aids, Bible History &c.

BLAIKIE (Rev. W. G.), **D.D.—BIBLE GEOGRAPHY.** With colored Maps. 16mo, cloth, 50 cts.

—— **BIBLE HISTORY,** in connection with the General History of the World, with Notices of Scripture Localities, and Sketches of Social and Religious Life. 12mo, cloth, $1.50.

COMPER GRAY (James).—**CLASS AND DESK** (The). A Manual for Sunday School Teachers. 4 vols. 12mo, cloth, $5.00; or sold separately, each, $1.25, namely:
Vol. 1. The Old Testament—Genesis to Esther.
Vol. 2. The Old Testament—Job to Malachi.
Vol. 3. The New Testament—The Gospels.
Vol. 4. The New Testament— The Epistles.

DICTIONARY OF SCRIPTURE PROPER NAMES, with their Pronunciations and Explanations. 16mo, paper covers, 13 cts. 16mo, cloth limp, 25 cts.

EDERSHEIM (Dr.).—**THE TEMPLE,** Its Ministry and Services. Small 4to, gilt edges, $2.50.

GREEN (Rev. S. G.).—**LECTURES TO CHILDREN ON** SCRIPTURE DOCTRINES. 32mo, cloth, 50 cts.

GROSER (W. H.).—**BIBLE MONTHS;** Or, The Seasons in Palestine as Illustrative of Scripture. Illustrated. 16mo, cloth, 25 cts.

—— **OUR WORK.** Four Lectures on the Principles and Practice of Sunday School Teaching. 18mo, cloth, 25 cts.

HELPS TO THE STUDY OF THE BIBLE, Containing the Notes, Tables, Index, Concordance, Maps, &c., &c., in the "OXFORD TEACHERS' BIBLE." 16mo, cloth, 75 cts.

JOSEPHUS' COMPLETE WORKS. Translated by W. Whiston, M.A. 8vo, cloth, $1.75.

NEW COMPANION TO THE BIBLE for Bible Classes, etc. Maps. 12mo, cloth, $1.25.

PHILIPS' SCRIPTURE ATLAS. 32mo, paper covers, 25 cts.

TREASURY OF SCRIPTURE KNOWLEDGE. 500,000 Scripture references and parallel passages from Canne, Brown, Blayney, Scott, etc., etc. 16mo, Turkey morocco, gilt edges, $5.00.

—

THOMAS NELSON AND SONS, 42 BLEECKER STREET, NEW YORK.

Selected List of Sunday School Books.

JUVENILES, &c.,

PUBLISHED BY T. NELSON & SONS.

ADA AND GERTY; Or, Hand in Hand Heavenward. By Louisa M. Gray. 12mo, cloth extra, beveled, $1.50.

AFAR IN THE FOREST; Or, Pictures of Life and Scenery in the Wilds of Canada. By Mrs. Traill. With colored frontispiece and vignette and many illustrations. 16mo, cloth extra, $1.00.

A. L. O. E.—FLORA; Or, Self-Deception. Illustrated. 12mo, cloth extra, gilt edges, $1.25.

ANNALS OF THE POOR. By the Rev. Leigh Richmond, M.A. 32mo, cloth extra, beveled, with illustrations, 50 cts.; 18mo, cloth extra, beveled, with tinted illustrations, 75 cts.; 12mo, cloth, chromo side, with numerous illustrations, $1.25.; 12mo, cloth, chromo side, gilt edges, with numerous illustrations, $1.50.

BECKWITH (General)—**HIS LIFE AND LABORS AMONG THE WALDENSES OF PIEDMONT.** By J. P. Meille, Pastor of the Waldensian Church in Turin. With an Introductory Notice by the late Rev. Wm. Arnot. 12mo, cloth, $1.25.

BRIGHTWELL (C. L.).—**LIVES OF LABOR**; Or, Incidents in the Career of Eminent Naturalists and Celebrated Travelers. By author of "Above Rubies," etc. Colored plates. 12mo, cloth extra, $1.50.

BUNYAN'S PILGRIM'S PROGRESS. 18mo, cloth, beveled, tinted illustrations, 75 cts.; 12mo, cloth extra, beveled, $1.00.

CITY AND CASTLE (The). A Story of the Reformation in Switzerland. By Annie Lucas. 12mo, cloth, $2.00.

CROWN OF GLORY (The); Or, "Faithful Unto Death." A Scottish Story of Martyr Times. By the author of "Little Hazel, the King's Messenger," etc. 12mo, cloth extra, $1.00.

CUPPLES (Mrs. George).—**FABLES.** Illustrated by Stories from Real Life. With numerous woodcuts. 18mo, cloth extra. First series, 75 cts.; Second series, 75 cts.

—— **MAMMA'S STORIES ABOUT DOMESTIC PETS.** Fully illustrated. 18mo, cloth extra, 75 cts.

—— **MY PRETTY SCRAP-BOOK**; Or, Picture Pages and Pleasant Stories for Little Readers. With illustration on every page. 18mo, cloth, 50 cts.

—— **SHADOWS ON THE SCREEN**; Or, an Evening with the Children. With illustration on every page. 18mo, cloth, 50 cts.

Selected List of Sunday School Books.

CUPPLES (Mrs. George).—**STORY OF OUR DOLL.** Large Type, 40 illustrations. 16mo, cloth, illuminated side, 60 cts.

——**STORY OF MISS DOLLIKINS** (The). With colored frontispiece, vignette, and 47 engravings. Oblong 24mo, illuminated side, 75 cts.

——**WALKS AND TALKS WITH GRANDPAPA.** With illustration on every page. 18mo, cloth, 50 cts.

DOUDNEY (Sarah).—**GREAT SALTERNS.** Illustrated. 12mo, cloth extra, gilt edges, $1.75.

EARLY GENIUS, As Illustrated by Bacon, Galileo, Newton, Cimabue, Giotto, Michael Angelo, Julius II., etc. By the author of "Success in Life," etc. Finely illustrated. 16mo, cloth extra, $1.50.

FALL OF JERUSALEM, AND THE ROMAN CONQUEST OF JUDEA. Illustrated. 18mo, cloth extra, 75 cts.

GALILEO, THE ASTRONOMER OF PISA. Colored frontispiece. 18mo, cloth, 50 cts.

GAUSSEN, (Prof. L.).—**WORLD'S BIRTHDAY** (The). A book for the young. Translated by Mrs. CAMPBELL OVERON. With colored plates. 16mo, cloth, $1.25.

GOOD OUT OF EVIL. A Tale for Children. By Mrs. SURR, author of "Sea-Birds and the Story of their Lives," etc. With 32 illustrations. 16mo, cloth extra, 75 cts.

HAPPY HOLIDAYS AT WOODLEIGH HOUSE; Or, Aunt Elsie and her Guests. 8 tinted illustrations. 16mo, cloth extra, $1.25.

HERSCHELS (Story of the). A Family of Astronomers. Colored frontispiece. 18mo, cloth, 50 cents.

HOLY WELL (The). An Irish Story. With colored frontispiece. 18mo, cloth extra, 25 cts.

IN THE FAR EAST. A Narrative of Exploration and Adventure in Cochin-China, Cambodia, Laos and Siam. 16mo, cloth extra, many illustrations, 75 cts.

KANE (Dr.), **THE ARCTIC HERO.** A Narrative of his Adventures and Explorations in the Polar Regions. By M. JONES. Fully illustrated. 16mo, cloth extra, $1.00.

KIRBY (Mary and Elizabeth).—**AUNT MARTHA'S CORNER** CUPBOARD. Stories about Tea, Coffee, Sugar, Honey, etc. With colored frontispiece, vignette, and numerous woodcuts. 12mo, cloth extra, $1.00.

THOMAS NELSON AND SONS, 42 BLEECKER STREET, NEW YORK.

Gift Books, Juveniles, Rewards, &c.

LEONIE; Or, Light Out of Darkness; and, **WITHIN IRON WALLS;** A Tale of the Siege of Paris. Twin Stories of the Franco-German War. By ANNIE LUCAS. 12mo, cloth extra, $2.00.

LITTLE ROBINSON OF PARIS; Or, The Triumph of Industry. From the French by LUCY LANDON. Tinted frontispiece and vignette, 18mo, cloth, $1.00.

LITTLE SNOWDROP AND HER GOLDEN CASKET. By the author of "Little Hazel," etc. With colored frontispiece and vignette. 12mo, cloth extra, $1.00.

MASTER AND SERVANT; Or, Richard Owen's Choice. By Mrs. LAMB. 18mo, cloth limp, gilt edges, 10 cts.

MERCHANT ENTERPRISE; Or, Pictures of the History of Commerce from the Earliest Times. By J. HAMILTON FYFE. With illustrations. 12mo, cloth, $1.50.

MILLER (Mrs. Hugh).—**STORIES OF THE CAT,** and her Cousins, the Lion, the Tiger, and the Leopard. Colored frontispiece, and many illustrations. 18mo, cloth extra, 75 cts.

—— **STORIES OF THE DOG,** and His Cousins, the Wolf, the Jackal, and the Hyena. With Stories illustrating their place in the Animal World. Illustrated. 18mo, cloth extra, 75 cts.

NELLY'S TEACHERS, AND WHAT THEY LEARNED. A Story for the Young. By KATE THORNE. 12mo, cloth extra, $1.50.

NEBULÆ AND COMETS. Colored frontispiece and vignette, and numerous illustrations. 16mo, cloth, 50 cts.

NOBLE WOMEN (Stories of the Lives of). By W. H. DAVENPORT ADAMS. 12mo, cloth, $1.25.

NO CROSS, NO CROWN; Or, The Dark Year of Dundee. A Tale of the Scottish Reformation, By the author of "Spanish Brothers." Illustrated. 12mo, cloth, $1.50.

PAULL (M. A.).—**VIVIANS OF WOODIFORD;** Or, True Hearts make Happy Homes. By the author of "Tim's Troubles," etc. Illustrated. 12mo, cloth, $1.50.

PENDOWER. A Story of Cornwall, in the Time of Henry the Eighth. By M. FILLEUL. 12mo, cloth extra, $2.00.

PLANETARY SYSTEM (The). Colored frontispiece and vignette, with numerous illustrations. 18mo, cloth, 50 cts.

Sunday School Books, Gift Books,

JUVENILES, REWARDS, &c.

PORTER (Rev. J. L.), A.M.—**GIANT CITIES OF BASHAN** (The), and Syria's Holy Places. Illustrated. 12mo, cloth, $1.50.

SEA AND THE SEA-SHORE (The). Lessons in the Study of Nature and Natural History. With numerous engravings. 12mo, cloth extra, $1.00.

SNOWDROP; Or, the Adventures of a White Rabbit. With colored frontispiece and vignette, and twenty illustrations. 16mo, cloth extra, $1.00.

SPANISH BROTHERS. A Tale of the Sixteenth Century. By the author of "Dark Year of Dundee." 12mo, cloth, $2.00.

STARS (The). Colored frontispiece and vignette, and numerous illustrations. 18mo, cloth. 50 cts.

STORY OF BENVENUTO CELLINI, THE ITALIAN GOLDSMITH. Colored frontispiece and vignette. 18mo, cloth extra, 50 cts.

STORY OF SIR HUMPHREY DAVY AND THE IN- VENTION OF THE SAFETY LAMP. Colored frontispiece and vignette. 18mo, cloth, 50 cts.

SUN AND MOON—Their Physical Character, Appearance and Phenomena. Colored frontispiece and vignette, and numerous illustrations. 18mo, cloth, 50 cts.

SWEDISH TWINS (The). A Tale for the Young. By the author of "The Babes in the Basket." 18mo, cloth extra, illustrated, 75 cts.

THRESHOLD OF LIFE (The). A Book of Illustrations and Lessons for the Encouragement and Counsel of Youth. By W. H. DAVENPORT ADAMS. 12mo, cloth, illustrated, $1.50.

TROT'S LETTERS TO HER DOLL. By MARY E. BROMFIELD. With beautiful colored frontispiece and vignette. 12mo, cloth extra, $1.00.

UNDER THE OAKS; Or, Won by Love. By AUTHOR OF "LITTLE HAZEL," etc. Colored frontispiece and vignette. 12mo, cloth extra, $1.00.

UNDER THE SOUTHERN CROSS. A Tale of the New World. By the author of "Spanish Brothers." 12mo, cloth, $2.00.

WHICH IS MY LIKENESS? Or, Seeing Ourselves as We See Others. By COUSIN KATE. With tinted plates. 12mo, cloth extra, $1.50.

WHITE-ROCK COVE (The). A Tale for the Young. With six colored plates. 12mo, cloth extra, gilt edges, $1.50.

THOMAS NELSON AND SONS, 42 BLEECKER STREET, NEW YORK.